Cowboy Charlie was back for a repeat performance.

His appearance this morning was rumpled, and he needed a shave. But so what? Despite Cassie's bad mood, she'd have had to be comatose not to observe how to-drool-over sexy the man was.

His sun-streaked hair flopped on his forehead. That crooked smile deepened the laugh lines around his Paul Newman eyes. He was tall, and slim, and sturdy, and possessed more animal charisma than ought to be allowed.

She'd half convinced herself that she'd dreamed him up the night before, some combination of stress and overactive imagination at work.

There went that theory....

Dear Reader,

Have you started your spring cleaning yet? If not, we have a great motivational plan: For each chore you complete, reward yourself with one Silhouette Romance title! And with the standout selection we have this month, you'll be finished reorganizing closets, steaming carpets and cleaning behind the refrigerator in record time!

Take a much-deserved break with the exciting new ROYALLY WED: THE MISSING HEIR title, *In Pursuit of a Princess,* by Donna Clayton. The search for the missing St. Michel heir leads an undercover princess straight into the arms of a charming prince. Then escape with Diane Pershing's SOULMATES addition, *Cassie's Cowboy.* Could the dreamy hero from her daughter's bedtime stories be for real?

Lugged out and wiped down the patio furniture? Then you deserve a double treat with Cara Colter's *What Child Is This?* and Belinda Barnes's *Daddy's Double Due Date.* In Colter's tender tearjerker, a tiny stranger reunites a couple torn apart by tragedy. And in Barnes's warm romance, a bachelor who isn't the "cootchie-coo" type discovers he's about to have twins!

You're almost there! Once you've rounded up every last dust bunny, you're really going to need some fun. In Terry Essig's *Before You Get to Baby...* and Sharon De Vita's *A Family To Be,* childhood friends discover that love was always right next door. De Vita's series, SADDLE FALLS, moves back to Special Edition next month.

Even if you skip the spring cleaning this year, we hope you don't miss our books. We promise, this is one project you'll love doing.

Happy reading!

Mary-Theresa Hussey
Senior Editor

Please address questions and book requests to:
Silhouette Reader Service
U.S.: 3010 Walden Ave., P.O. Box 1325, Buffalo, NY 14269
Canadian: P.O. Box 609, Fort Erie, Ont. L2A 5X3

Cassie's Cowboy

DIANE PERSHING

Published by Silhouette Books

America's Publisher of Contemporary Romance

If you purchased this book without a cover you should be aware that this book is stolen property. It was reported as "unsold and destroyed" to the publisher, and neither the author nor the publisher has received any payment for this "stripped book."

To Karen Amarillas, for her friendship and expertise in rodeo lore. And to Ken, who—although he refuses to wear boots and Stetson—still fits my definition of a hero.

 SILHOUETTE BOOKS

ISBN 0-373-19584-2

CASSIE'S COWBOY

Copyright © 2002 by Diane Pershing

All rights reserved. Except for use in any review, the reproduction or utilization of this work in whole or in part in any form by any electronic, mechanical or other means, now known or hereafter invented, including xerography, photocopying and recording, or in any information storage or retrieval system, is forbidden without the written permission of the editorial office, Silhouette Books, 300 East 42nd Street, New York, NY 10017 U.S.A.

All characters in this book have no existence outside the imagination of the author and have no relation whatsoever to anyone bearing the same name or names. They are not even distantly inspired by any individual known or unknown to the author, and all incidents are pure invention.

This edition published by arrangement with Harlequin Books S.A.

® and TM are trademarks of Harlequin Books S.A., used under license. Trademarks indicated with ® are registered in the United States Patent and Trademark Office, the Canadian Trade Marks Office and in other countries.

Visit Silhouette at www.eHarlequin.com

Printed in U.S.A.

Books by Diane Pershing

Silhouette Romance

Cassie's Cowboy #1584

Silhouette Intimate Moments

While You Were Sleeping #863
The Tough Guy and the Toddler #928

Silhouette Yours Truly

First Date: Honeymoon
Third Date's the Charm

Harlequin Duets

Hot Copy

DIANE PERSHING

cannot remember a time when she didn't have her nose buried in a book. As a child, she would cheat the bedtime curfew by snuggling under the covers with her teddy bear, a flashlight and a forbidden (read "grown-up") novel. Her mother warned her that she would ruin her eyes, but so far, they still work. Diane has had many careers—singer, actress, film critic, disc jockey, TV writer, to name a few. Currently she divides her time between writing romances and doing voice-overs. (You can hear her as "Poison Ivy" on the *Batman* cartoon.) She lives in Los Angeles, and promises she is only slightly affected. Her two children, Morgan Rose and Ben, have just completed college, and Diane looks forward to writing and acting until she expires, or people stop hiring her, whichever comes first. She loves to hear from readers, so please write to her at P.O. Box 67424, Los Angeles, CA 90067.

Dear Reader,

When I was young, any girl worth her salt had a crush on cowboys…and their horses, of course. On my block you were either for Roy Rogers or Gene Autry. The occasional Hopalong Cassidy booster showed up, but we paid them no mind (if you are too young to know who I'm talking about, trust me, you missed a great time). I was firmly in the Roy camp. Last year, during a difficult family period, I'd been trying unsuccessfully to flesh out a story idea about a pair of truly ugly magical eyeglasses. One night I had a dream in which Roy showed up and told me not to fret my pretty little head, that he and Trigger would take care of my problems for a while. Sigh. It was a lovely dream. Upon awakening, the two ideas meshed, and *Cassie's Cowboy* was born. Giddyup!

Diane Pershing

Chapter One

"...and then the bad man with the long, smelly mustache tightened the ropes that bound the hands of Sally and her small child, Missy. Both of his prisoners were very, very frightened, and they would have liked to scream for help but the bad man had put handkerchiefs over their mouths, so all they could do was make noises like *murfle hurfle pelp!* Suddenly, from over the horizon there appeared a stranger in a Stetson—"

"Cowboy Charlie!" Trish said happily, clapping her hands.

"Yes, my love," Cassie said, and went on. "Here came Cowboy Charlie, galloping on Felicity, his six-guns blazing. With an *oomph!* and a *pow!* he kicked the bad man so he fell and rolled over and over and over, down the mountain. Then Charlie swooped up the woman and her child onto his horse, and the three of them rode off into the sunset, to safety."

"Oh, Mommy," Trish sighed, snuggling back

against her pillow and pulling her covers up under her chin. "That was so good. It's my favorite story."

Cassie Nevins smiled warmly at her seven-year-old daughter. "You always say that, no matter which story I tell you," she teased, then kissed her child's soft cheek. "Good night, baby," she said, gathering her notebook and pens as she left the room. Their nightly ritual was done, the story was told, accompanied, as usual, by one or two pen-and-ink sketches. The drawings she'd come up with this particular evening weren't bad, even if she did say so herself. She'd really gotten the look of Cowboy Charlie tonight.

He was the Old West heroic type, from the days before *Star Wars,* when kids used to worship cowboys and the horses they rode. Tall, slim but muscular, his legs slightly bowed from years riding the range, his strong face lined by days spent squinting into the sun. He wore chaps and boots with jangling spurs and a leather vest—all the classic paraphernalia—and rode a magnificent chestnut named Felicity. Cassie was particularly pleased with the arch of the horse's neck in tonight's drawing. And she'd finally captured the look in Charlie's nearly turquoise-blue eyes—reliable, amused. Manly. She was getting better and better at this.

After she closed the door to her daughter's room, Cassie paused, removed her brand-new reading glasses and rubbed her tired eyes. She contemplated getting a snack, as she'd hardly eaten her dinner. But she couldn't summon up the energy. She supposed she could go into her small office and stare at the bills there. But that would be all she'd be able to do, she thought wryly—stare at them. She sure couldn't pay them.

Maybe she could indulge in a hot bath. Had the water bill been paid? Yes. Good, then. A soothing soak, just the thing to loosen tense muscles and strained eyes.

With a huge sigh, she found herself staring at the glasses she held in her hand. Boy, were they ugly, she thought, then chuckled. Past ugly, to be sure. Hideous. Bright turquoise frames with fan-shaped edges, dotted with inlaid rhinestones. So tasteless, so tacky. But they hadn't cost her a cent; therefore, they were beautiful.

She'd been getting headaches lately when she read, and kindly old Doc Slater, her optometrist, had told her the week before that she needed reading glasses. As he'd had an inkling of her financial situation, he'd offered the frames to her, free. They were an extra pair in a shipment, he'd told her, and waved off her effusive thanks. She'd picked them up this morning.

As she headed for the bath, Cassie rubbed her thumb along the glasses' earpiece. She was not only tired, she was rapidly on the way to being downright grumpy. And, despite her usual sunny outlook, she was beginning to sense the edges of panic. She needed money, she needed hope, she needed help, none of which were in sight.

Actually, what she needed now was a rescuer, of the knight-in-shining-armor variety.

No, forget the knight. What she needed was a cowboy, one of the good guys, as opposed to the bad guys. How very nice it would be if Cowboy Charlie would come along and make all her troubles disappear.

Right, she thought with a rueful smile. And he could bring the Tooth Fairy with him.

She turned on the hot water tap, then began to unbutton her blouse. Her hands paused as she thought she heard a noise. What was it? Some kind of knocking? Frowning, she turned the water off and listened. Yes, there it went again. Someone was knocking at her front door.

Putting on her glasses, she glanced at her watch. Who could it be at nine at night? Swallowing down the automatic fear reaction of a woman who lived alone with her child, she hurried downstairs before whoever it was knocked again. She went to the door and peered through the peephole.

In the yellow glow cast by the porch light, she could make out the figure of a man. Not just any man, but—

Cassie gasped as her hand automatically flew to cover her pounding heart. Unless she was completely mistaken, standing there, big as life, was none other than...Cowboy Charlie!

Charlie wasn't real clear on just what had happened. Last thing he remembered, he was riding Felicity along the stretch they called Sagebrush Plain. He'd been admiring the way the setting sun was coating the far-off mountains with the darnedest colors— all purples and reds and golds—and thinking about the juicy steak he intended to have when he got back to camp, when all at once he swore he heard the sound of a woman sighing.

And not just an itty-bitty sigh, but a gigantic sigh, one that echoed and echoed and got louder and louder until he had to cover his ears. And then, *Whoosh!* there was a new sound, a roar twice as big as the sound of a hurricane. Suddenly, he felt his body being lifted and hurled through some kind of sideways tornado. Round and round he twisted till he could barely catch a breath. And then, just as suddenly, he was on land again, feet first and standing upright.

On a strange porch, facing a strange door.

And knocking on that door, because that seemed to be the obvious thing to do.

Now a woman was opening that door, but keeping the screen door between them closed.

"Ma'am?" he said, removing his hat and smoothing back his hair, then settling it back on his head. He was still breathing pretty heavily from his trip, but that didn't affect his eyesight. No, sir.

She was just about the cutest thing he'd seen in a long while. Little, not a bit over five feet, he bet. Her head was all over short brown curls, and her eyes were brown too, chocolate-colored and large. Right now they peered suspiciously at him over the top of the strangest looking pair of spectacles he'd ever seen and which were perched on the tip of her small nose.

"Good evening," he said politely, when she seemed disobliged to say anything welcoming.

The woman checked to make sure the lock was on the screen door, then crossed her arms over her chest. "And just who are you supposed to be?" She had a low, raspy-sounding voice, which didn't really go with the small, compact body, but it sure did sound womanly, and it sure did set up a little male appreciation-type humming in his blood.

"I figured you would know, ma'am."

"Why don't you tell me, anyway?" One of her eyebrows was raised, mistrustful-like, as though he was trying to sell her a steer for stud work.

"Cowboy Charlie, of course," he said with a smile

that usually melted any chill a lady might be sending out. "You can call me just plain Charlie, if you'd like."

"Mm-hmm," she said, that pretty little mouth of hers set in a real disbelieving line. "And just how did you get here, 'just plain Charlie'?" She spoke his name like it was something he'd made up.

Which was strange, because she'd been the one to come up with it.

"Well, I was doing what I always do, you know, riding the range on my horse, looking for adventures and folks who need rescuing, and the next thing I knew I was here. Felicity didn't make it, though."

"Felicity."

"My horse. You know. You named him."

"Him?"

"Yes, ma'am. Felicity's a he, a gelding actually. But I figured you didn't know that when you thought up his moniker."

"Oh." Her eyes widened in surprise. "No I didn—" She cut herself off in mid-sentence then shook her head. She fixed her gaze on him for a long moment, like she was trying to figure out a puzzle. "I'll say this much. You're good."

"Excuse me?"

"Whoever sent you, they chose well. You're a dead ringer for him."

Charlie was feeling just a bit confused. "*You* sent me, ma'am."

"Did I?" That one suspicious eyebrow shot up again. "And just where did I get you from? I mean, exactly where is that range you were riding on?"

He wondered why she was testing him this way,

but figured he'd find out soon enough. "Well, it's kind of hard to explain. May I come in?"

He reached for the door handle.

"You may not," she fairly snapped at him. "I don't let strangers into my house."

"Oh."

He thought a bit, pushed his hat back and scratched his head. Then, figuring he might be standing here for a while, he leaned an elbow against the door frame and crossed one booted foot over the other.

A cricket nearby set to chirping, which made Charlie feel a little less strange. There were crickets where he came from, too. And porches, and screen doors—although they had wooden frames back home, not iron ones like this one.

"Okay, now, where is that range?" he repeated, then lifted one shoulder in a shrug. "Well, that's a little complicated. See, there's a kind of a...well, a place, a section..." He'd never had to put it into words before. "Not here, I mean not here, in your world..."

"So you're from Heaven?" Now she was being downright sarcastic. With someone else, he might have bristled at her attitude, but he figured this was one part of some kind of test he was being put through, so he'd just have to go along as best he could.

Besides, darned if she wasn't the cutest, sassiest gal he'd seen in a while. Then there was the way her blouse was open a ways, and how that piece of white lace that peeked out from the opening more than hinted at a sweet pair of—

Charlie coughed and brought himself back to her question. "Heaven? No, not really. But that's as good a name as any. It's this special world for what you call fictional characters. We got Oliver Twist back there and Batman, and Romeo and Juliet—poor things are always sighing at each other. And we all sort of...well, kinda live there. Until we're sent for, I guess," he finished with a grin. "Which, I figure, is what happened this time."

Until we're sent for.

The minute the stranger said those words, Cassie felt an icy shiver skitter up and down her spine, and its effect was terrifying. Mostly because she was starting to believe this guy. No! She shook her head. No. She must be in a dream. Or the butt of some bizarre joke.

But she'd meant what she'd said: the man was good. Really a pro. *Exactly* as she'd pictured Cowboy Charlie, *exactly* as she'd drawn him, down to the small dimple on one side of his mouth and the way his sun-streaked hair flapped attractively over his forehead.

Truth be told, she'd always been a little in love with her creation, fictional though he was. She'd invented him not just for Trish but for herself. A fantasy man, one with all the historically classic, manly characteristics. Strength. Trustworthiness. Protectiveness. A hard worker, honest and dependable.

And sexy, too. That part had definitely been for her, not Trish.

A sexy man for her dream life, which was a far cry from the difficult, complex, real world she inhabited day to day.

A fantasy man was the only kind she'd allow entrance into her life. After her late husband, Teddy—a sweet, well-intentioned-but-unreliable man—Cassie had been in no hurry for anyone new to love. Thus Cowboy Charlie: the perfect—not in real life but perfect nevertheless—classic hero.

Gazing at him now, she had to fight the sudden urge to invite him in, whoever he was. He was as appealing as anything she'd seen in a long, long time.

But good sense took over. One did not open one's door to a strange man. Especially not at night. And not with her precious daughter sleeping upstairs.

Still, he wasn't the least bit threatening, and Cassie had pretty good instincts that way. There was something comforting about his presence. He felt like...Cowboy Charlie, down to that scar at the edge of his right eyebrow, the one he'd gotten in the tussle with a knife-wielding bank robber down in Baja.

No! This time the icy shiver that zipped through her veins made her jump. Charlie hadn't run into a knife-wielding bank robber in Baja, not in reality.

Charlie was fictional! She had made up that story, made up all the Cowboy Charlie stories. Had, in fact, made up the man who was standing here now, big as life on her porch and chatting away in his lazy, masculine drawl, easy and likable.

And achingly familiar.

Cassie found her body leaning forward, as though she were being drawn to him. With only the screen door separating them, she could swear she could smell him, and what she took in was a heady mixture of healthy sweat, old leather and pipe tobacco. It was an intoxicating blend.

Wait a minute. Pipe tobacco? Oh that's right, in a couple of early stories, she'd had Charlie lighting up a pipe as he sat around the campfire with some of his buddies, so that made sense. But she'd cut out the pipe in the later tales, not wanting to send any kind of tobacco-as-soothing message to her daughter. Apparently, *this* Cowboy Charlie hadn't gotten the word.

Help, she thought weakly, although she wasn't sure who the plea was aimed toward. She had to stop this nonsense, pull back from the spell cast by the stranger.

Propping her hands on her hips, she glared at this man, this fake Cowboy Charlie. "Enough," she said firmly. "The truth now. Who sent you?"

He frowned, then removed his elbow from the door frame and stood up straight. "You did, ma'am," he said politely. "You're Miz Nevins, right? Cassie Nevins?"

The woman's eyes narrowed, but she nodded, so Charlie went on. "I'm not really sure, but those spectacles? The ones on the end of your nose? I think they mighta had something to do with it." He shook his head. "See, this is as much a surprise to me as it is to you. Now, I've heard tales, about others who've left, you know, and it was because they were needed, real bad. They were sent for because that person who needed them? Well, that person did something to bring it about, to...make it happen. I'm not real clear on this, as I said, but in the back of my head, there's this idea that it's connected to your spectacles."

When Cassie continued to stare at him with an expression of pure confusion, he went on talking, hoping he'd light on the words that would help her understand, so she could be more peaceful than she seemed.

"Maybe it's something like Aladdin did—we got him back home, too. Like rubbing a magic bottle? Or when you wish on a star? You must have done something like that." He shrugged. "I'm sorry. I wish I knew more. I'm kind of new at this myself."

"I did something?"

He nodded. "I'm pretty sure that before I left, well, before I was lifted, I guess you'd call it, out of my world and into this one, I had a picture in my head of—" he pointed "—those spectacles." He finished his explanation with an apologetic smile that made his eyebrows turn up at the bridge of his nose. He'd done the best he could; now he'd wait to see if she understood.

As the cowboy pointed, Cassie realized she was still wearing the unstylish turquoise reading glasses. She pulled them off, folded them up and stuck them in the pocket of her blouse. It was then she grasped the fact that when she'd been preparing for her bath, she'd unbuttoned her blouse halfway down her chest.

Which was how it had remained, for the entire conversation with this man. Dear God.

Feeling heat suffuse her cheeks, she quickly remedied the situation, but had some trouble meeting his gaze as she did.

"They sure are funny looking, aren't they?" the cowboy said.

Her head snapped up. "What's funny looking?"

"The spectacles."

"Oh, yes. A true laugh riot," Cassie muttered.

"Maybe they're magic. You wished I was real, and I guess you really wished hard, because—" he spread his palms "—here I am."

You wished I was real. His simple words stunned her once again. Her previous seminaked state forgotten, Cassie could only stare at the man on her porch. Surely this couldn't be. He was spinning a yarn, yes that was it. That had to be it. He'd seen the ugly glasses perched on her nose and had come up with this whole, ludicrous explanation.

Except how did he know about the wish she'd made not five minutes ago, in jest of course. How could he know? Did he read minds? Was that it?

She closed her eyes and inhaled a deep breath. She was dreaming, she told herself. She had to be. Even though the man on her porch, chatting easily like an old friend, seemed to be flesh and blood, down to the smell of pipe tobacco.

"So, I reckon I'll be with you for a while," he went on. "Until I finish helping you out, of course."

She opened her eyes again, but she was struck speechless, so all she could do was stare at him and shake her head in wonder.

"And I sure don't mean to be rude," he went on, "but I had to travel quite a far piece, and I have a powerful thirst. May I trouble you for a glass of water?"

He waited for her answer, but Cassie was unable to say anything at the moment.

Deterred not in the least, he went on. "Are you sure I can't come in? I'm plum tuckered out. I can bunk down on your davenport, if you'd like." He spread his hands and grinned the Cowboy Charlie grin she'd invented for him, based on the way Brad Pitt looked when he was feeling cocky. It was a smile that invited you to be in on the joke with him, the one that always brought sunshine to a dreary outlook.

She shook her head until she was sure her brains were back in place. Then she stood ramrod straight.

Enough!

Either he was insane or she was. Either way, it was time to end this.

"Listen to me, Cowboy Charlie, or whoever you are," she said with newfound strength and purpose. "If you're fictional, you don't get tired and you don't need any water."

"But—"

She refused to let him continue. "And no, you cannot stay here," she added indignantly, positive that someone had slipped her a hallucinogenic drug or that she was in a deep dream state and would wake in the morning, back to her old self again. "In fact," she added for emphasis, "good night!"

Ignoring the confused look on the stranger's face, she closed the door and double locked it, clicked off the porch light and stomped up the stairs.

There! she thought. *That was telling him!*

She was probably sleepwalking—it was the only explanation that made sense—but it was time to seek the safety of her bed.

In the morning he'd be gone for sure.

Chapter Two

The phone rang, followed by Trish complaining, followed by a knock at the front door. All she needed, Cassie thought, on the verge of screaming, was for a bomb to go off. Then her life would be complete.

Setting the bowl of cereal down in front of her daughter with a bang, she picked up the phone and barked into it, "Hold on." She glared resolutely at Trish. "You know I can't hear you when you whine."

"But I don't like oatmeal, Mommy," her daughter whined, and pushed the cereal away.

"It's all we have this morning, so get over it. Yes?" she said into the phone, then pushed the bowl of cereal back before her daughter. "Not interested," she said to the telemarketer.

"That's a shame," an overly bright young voice replied, "because—"

Cassie hung up before she got to hear about the shame. "Where is it written," she said to no one in particular, "that just because I have a telephone I'm fair game?"

"Do I have to eat this, Mommy?" Trish asked again.

"You betcha."

Cassie was aware that she was acting and sounding cranky. But it had been a rough night, she had a headache that took up all available space behind her eye sockets—including her brain, she was sure—and the bright sunlight pouring in through the missing slats of the kitchen window blinds was directed straight at her eyes, as though she'd been purposely targeted by the sun gods.

She poured herself another cup of coffee and took a slug. "I overslept and need to get dressed for work, honey," she went on, forcing her voice to be more gentle, "so eat up before the car pool gets here."

"But—"

"No buts. Do it."

Insistent knocking at the door made Cassie jump. Oops. She'd managed to forget that someone had already knocked once, just seconds ago. She glanced at the wall clock. It was ten minutes early for the car pool, but Helen Wasserman, whose turn it was today, was one of those chirpy, "better early than late" type-A personalities that Cassie positively loathed.

"Eat," she ordered her pouting daughter. "I'll tell Helen she'll just have to wait a couple of minutes."

Determined to check her testiness before she got to the door—after all, it wouldn't do to unload on the poor woman whose only sin was a terror of being tardy—Cassie hurried to the front door. Before she opened it, she made sure her robe was tied. Then, forcing a broad smile onto unwilling cheek muscles, she pulled open the door.

The smile left her face right away. In fact, her mouth dropped open, wide as the door, at the sight on her porch.

It was him. Again.

Or still.

Cowboy Charlie, in person, back for a repeat performance.

His appearance this morning was rumpled, and he needed a shave. But so what? Despite her bad mood, she'd have had to be comatose not to observe how to-drool-over sexy the man was.

His sun-streaked hair flopped on his forehead. That crooked smile deepened the laugh lines around his Paul Newman eyes. He was tall and slim and sturdy, and possessed more animal charisma than ought to be allowed.

She'd half convinced herself that she'd dreamed him up the night before, some combination of stress and overactive imagination at work. Cassie sighed. Well, there went that theory.

Whoever he was, he was no apparition, that was for sure. One of her friends, that had to be the explanation. A few of them knew all about her Cowboy Charlie stories. Sandy, or Margie, or some other well-meaning person had decided to play a little trick on her, bring a little fun into her stressful life. This, she decided, seemed like sound reasoning, even if the likelihood of finding an exact replica of her Charlie—as exact as this one was—had to be pretty remote.

But still, the whole thing had to be a joke. And she'd go along with the joke, by heaven, because Cassie had a sense of humor.

Like that she found herself relaxing in his easy-going, attractive presence. Not that whoever was responsible wasn't going to pay, big-time, she amended. Still, for the moment she'd play her part and have a little fun at the same time. And why not? After all, the man was, quite simply, impossible to resist.

Her mind made up, instead of taking his head off, when Charlie smiled, Cassie found herself smiling back.

"Morning," he said cheerfully. "How're we doing today?"

"We're just ducky," she said, chuckling. "And you?"

There, Charlie thought. He'd suspected that the lady's smile would warm up her pretty face, would bring that merry sparkle to her eyes, and darned if he hadn't been right. "I sure could use that drink, ma'am. I spent the night in that shed behind your house, and there wasn't any water that I could find."

"You slept in my garage?"

"Yes, ma'am."

She bit the edge of her lip, but he could tell she wasn't really upset anymore. She wore a long robe, one that outlined that cute little body of hers, letting him know that the curves he remembered from the night before were real. He wondered briefly if he was supposed to be noticing her body and the nice rasp of her voice, if that was part of his quest. But whether or not he was supposed to, he was a man, after all. Some things were not in his control.

Folding her arms over her chest, she asked, but with a smile, "Okay, truth time. Who sent you?"

Uh-oh. We're back to that again. Charlie pushed his hat back and scratched his head, trying to tamp down the small spurt of irritation her question aroused. "I thought we got that straightened out last night," he said, determined to be patient, even though his mouth felt like sawdust. "You did."

"Right. Okay, I sent for you." She sighed, shook her head. "But if I tell you I don't have time to play this morning as I'm running late, would you be willing to go back to wherever it is you came from?"

He removed his Stetson and smoothed back his hair, something he always did when he needed a moment to ponder a situation. "I'm not sure I can do that," he told her, setting the hat back on his head. "All I know is you called me, I'm here and I'm supposed to rescue you, and that's about it."

At the perplexed expression on her face, he added, with a shrug, "I'm sure sorry. I don't know any more than you do what the rules are. I'm afraid the whole thing isn't up to me. Or you. So, I figure we both better accept it and just get on with it."

"'Just get on with it,'" she repeated.

"Yes, ma'am."

She studied him for a while, seemed to be deciding something big, then, like that, she sighed, opened the screen door and stepped aside. "Put the guns down—" she pointed to his holster and six-shooters "—and then come on in."

"They aren't real bullets, you know."

"There are bullets in there?"

He popped open the chamber and peered inside. "Not anymore," he told her, taken aback by the fact. He twirled both empty chambers, to show her.

"Good. Put the guns down, anyway, all right? This is a gun-free household."

He did as she'd requested, removing his holster and

setting it down on a small bench by the door. Then he crossed the threshold just as she said, "The least I can do, I guess, is to offer you a glass of water. If Margie or Sandy or Rosa put you up to this, you're probably harmless, right?"

"Well, ma'am," he offered, "I don't know as I've ever been called harmless, exactly. But I know how to behave myself. My mamma made sure all us boys had manners."

"I'm sure she did. I'm Cassie, by the way."

"Yes, ma'am, I know."

It felt nice and cool inside and he was grateful. It was hotter than Hades out there already, even though it was only morning. He gazed down at her. My, she was a little one. Fiery, for all that, but still, little.

"And you can cut out the 'ma'am' stuff," she said, propping her hands on her hips. "I'm not old enough yet." Grinning one more time, she added, "Though I'm rapidly getting there."

She turned and he followed her, boots clicking and spurs jangling loudly as he trod her wooden floors. But he didn't really pay any attention to the sound, because he was watching the way her shapely hips moved inside her robe. And his nose was picking up the scent of—what? Some kind of spring flowers. Lilacs, maybe. It floated behind her and right into his nostrils. The scent of a woman. This woman. Cassie smelled downright *savory*.

In the kitchen a girl child sat at a small round table, making a face at a bowl of mush. She raised her head when her momma walked in with him following. Her eyes grew huge with wonder as she stared at him.

"Mommy!" she said. "It's Cowboy Charlie!"

"Morning, miss," he said with a tip of his hat.

"Mommy!" she squealed again, her high-pitched voice verging on affecting his hearing. The little girl stood, looking excitedly from him to her mother and back again. "It's Cowboy Charlie! He's here!"

"No, it's not him," Cassie answered, taking a glass from a shelf and turning on the tap. "Not really. Well, yes and no. Oh, heck." She shrugged her shoulders, seeming to surrender any attempt to make sense. "Whatever. Charlie, meet Trish."

He offered his hand to the child, who took it. "Pleased to make your acquaintance, Trish," he told her solemnly, but the little girl's face lit up with a grin that made her look just like a fairer-haired, rounder-faced version of her mother.

"Me, too. You're my hero."

"Trish, eat your oatmeal," Cassie said.

Indicating with her head that Charlie should sit across from her daughter, Cassie poured him a glass of water, then set it down in front of his chair. He was dying to drink and wouldn't have minded resting his feet, but he waited for her to take a seat.

Instead, she selected a cup from another shelf and poured what looked like coffee from a silver-colored machine on the counter next to the sink. "You like it black, right?"

"As tar."

"Sorry. It's strong, but not quite that strong."

A horn sounded outside. Cassie turned to her daughter, who was still grinning at Charlie. "That's your car pool, honey. I guess you don't have to eat your oatmeal after all, lucky you. Take some oatmeal cookies with you."

"But, Cowboy Charlie's here," the little girl said,

the sparkle in her eyes bright with happiness and wonder. "I want to stay."

"I'll be here when you get back, little lady," he told her.

"Mom?" Trish said with a squeak of joy that made him wince. "Will he be here?"

"We'll see," Cassie said.

At the exact same moment Charlie opined, with a wink, "I sure will."

The little girl looked from her mother to him, then decided to go with his answer. "Goody!" She clapped her hands. "Wait till I tell everyone!" She grabbed a few cookies from a jar on the counter, seized a small pack with straps from the back of her chair and ran out the door.

Frowning, Cassie set both cups of coffee down on the table. Alone at last. She noticed that Charlie waited to sit until she did, and wondered when was the last time anyone had displayed actual manners. It felt quaint...and kind of nice.

She watched as he downed the water quickly, his Adam's apple darting up and down with each gulp. His hands were deeply tanned, his fingers callused. As she sipped her coffee, she studied him, ignoring the attraction she felt toward him in an attempt at objectivity.

In the morning light he was even more the embodiment of Cowboy Charlie than he had appeared to be last night. Everything about him indicated that he worked with those sun-browned hands, that he spent days on the trail, in the open air. She wondered about his background, how much he was getting paid for this little impersonation, and frowned as she tried to think which of her friends had money for this kind of thing.

And why whoever it was had decided to play a trick on her in the first place.

"You shouldn't have said that to Trish," she admonished. "About your being here when she got home."

"Why not?"

"Because you'll get her hopes up. She thinks you're real, as opposed to me, who knows you aren't."

He frowned, obviously perplexed and just a little bit impatient with her. "I thought we'd gotten that all worked out last night. I *am* real. You can touch me if you'd like." He put his hand out toward her. "Flesh and blood, just like most men."

Not even close to most men, at least the ones I know, she could have said, but didn't. Instead she set her coffee cup down, then folded both arms across her chest.

"Look," she said firmly, "I may have some Irish heritage and my grandmother may have filled my head with tales of faeries, curses and Fate, but that was then, this is now. I'm a grown-up, and I rebel against being asked to accept some, some…creature of my imagination turning into flesh and blood reality. Okay? It isn't possible, it didn't happen, and that's it!"

There. If that didn't get through to him, she didn't know what would.

But he didn't react, not really, except for a slight tension around the jawline that disappeared almost as quickly as it had appeared. No, he just shrugged, sat there and drank down her coffee, a thoughtful look on his handsome, weather-beaten face.

Had she hurt his feelings? she wondered suddenly. Did he mind being called a creature? What in the world was going on? And, more immediate, what in the world was she going to do with him?

"Are you hungry or anything?" she found herself asking him, by way of soothing any feathers she might have ruffled. At once she was disgusted with herself. God, she was such a wuss. Every time she forced herself to act with firmness and strength, in the next moment, she usually wound up taking care of whoever she'd been firm and strong with.

"Don't bother yourself, ma'am—I mean, Cassie. I'll get myself some grub later on."

She reached behind her for the cookie jar. Setting it in front of her, she opened the top and handed him a couple of oatmeal cookies, which he accepted, she noticed.

"Thanks," he said, then gobbled them down, like someone who'd been deprived of food for a while. He really needed this impersonation job, she figured, wondering again at his background and what had brought him to this point.

Both cookies were disposed of in a matter of seconds, after which he said, "You're a real good baker."

"No I'm not. Other people bake. I shop. There's more, if you'd like. Or I can scramble up some eggs."

She began to rise, but he stayed her with a gesture. "No thank you. I meant what I said. I'll eat later. Now I need you to tell me what I can do for you."

He seemed so sincere, so earnest, she almost laughed, mainly because it crossed her mind that it would be nice if she *could* believe in fairy tales, in someone sent from another plane of existence to help her.

Maybe she had believed at Trish's age, but the early death of her mother, followed two years later by her father's death, had taken away her childhood long before it should have ended, along with any faith in either magic or fantasy. A maiden aunt had raised her to the best of her abilities, but she'd been a sour and strict woman. Cassie had left her home right after high school and had never gone back.

She'd met Teddy in junior college, at age nineteen, married him three months later, had Trish at twenty and been widowed at twenty-six, nearly two years ago.

Since then there had been no room for fairy tales, very little room for much of anything except the day-to-day struggle to just get by. So now this man in cowboy duds sat across from her, all earnestness and manners, asking what he could do for her?

The obvious first answer came to mind. Money would help. Her late husband, who had done enough dreaming for both of them, had always been into some kind of flaky financial scheme. In fact, he'd put the house up as collateral on the final project, something to do with windmills and solar power. It had failed, of course, as had all the others. After that, he'd been so distracted, he'd accidentally stepped into the path of a large truck and been mowed down like a weed.

Cassie hadn't had the luxury of weeping all the tears she'd felt inside; there was a five-year-old child to raise and bills to pay. There had been no insurance, no savings. Only debt. This small structure in the tiny town of Yatesboro, Nevada, twenty miles outside of Reno, was all that she and Trish had left, and every month they seemed on the verge of losing it.

There was never enough money, not for extras like ballet lessons for Trish or art classes for Cassie, so she could hone the skills to translate what she saw in her head onto paper. Her job at a local dress shop, while enjoyable enough, was not a high-paying one, but she had no training in anything that might bring in a better salary.

Short of winning the lottery—which she couldn't even afford to enter—she didn't see a way out.

Not that she'd given up hope, of course. She never did that, not even on grumpy mornings like this, not even metaphorically tied to the railroad tracks and the steam from the oncoming train filling the air above her. Somehow she'd survived tragic childhood losses with hope intact. It Isn't Over Till It's Over, was her motto.

But what she knew was that hope had to be based in reality, on what was *possible*. Not on dreams and what-ifs.

Not on fictional characters being brought to life.

Still, she wished, oh, how she wished, that this Cowboy Charlie was who he said he was, and that he could produce a small pot of gold for her needs.

But she didn't believe it, not for a second.

"Ma'am?" he said, bringing her back to the moment.

"That's Cassie," she reminded him again with a rueful smile as she rose from the table. "And I have to get dressed for work."

"Oh."

Rising, as well, Charlie sensed this wasn't a good

time to ask about his living arrangements. While he was doing whatever he was supposed to be doing, he'd have to settle for the garage, he supposed—it sure did seem the davenport was out. And the davenport wasn't even close to where he'd like to bunk down, which was right next to Cassie, in her own bed.

He drew in a sharp breath. Tarnation. He hadn't expected there to be these strong *feelings* when he looked at her, these bodily stirrings. It felt peculiar, somehow, to be experiencing so many potent sensations. There was a hankering for the woman, for sure; that one was at the top of the list. But there were other responses to her. Admiration for her spunk. A feeling of lightness in her presence, happiness almost. A need to protect her.

Then there were all these other human reactions—hunger, thirst, a need to sleep. Just yesterday he'd been fiction, but now he was real.

He didn't question it, just knew it. Still, it was all new, and he'd have some settling in to do, he figured.

Cassie didn't accept his human state, not yet. But she would. It was a fact: Cowboy Charlie had been granted temporary personhood. Along with that, he'd also been granted the knowledge that real life was much more complex than his fictional world.

Back home it was simple. The Code of the Old West was to act honorably, work hard, tell the truth and take responsibility. But that might not be enough here. Sure, he'd been sent to, as they'd have said back home, "help the widder woman."

But he wasn't back home. To do what he was supposed to do, he'd need to adapt and quickly. It wasn't only about life versus fiction, it was also about the fact that Cassie's century was a lot more complicated than his.

He watched as she took both coffee cups to the sink and placed them there. "You'll have to leave," she said, following it up quickly with, "Sorry. I don't mean to be rude, but I have to get to work and first I have to get dressed. Needless to say I'm not about to do that with you still here."

"Oh, surely, yes."

She walked him to the door. It made sense that she didn't want him in the house while she dressed—she didn't know him well enough. Not that he'd have minded watching her dress, with her permission, of course, but it looked like that wasn't in the cards.

She opened the front door. Bright sunshine flooded the entrance, and he remembered the heat outside. "Well then, I'll just wait for you on the porch, if that's okay."

She bit her bottom lip in consternation. "No, I don't think that's a good idea. I have a busy day, and I'm sure you have other things to do with your time. Okay?" She offered her hand. "It was nice meeting you."

Confused again, he took her hand in his. Small and soft, just like he'd imagined. Her skin felt good against his palm and so did the quick surge of desire that shot up his arm and began to spread elsewhere. That surely was one powerful reaction; too powerful.

Abruptly he dropped her hand, then tipped his hat. "Nice meeting you, too," he said, then walked out into the sunshine.

Cassie closed the door, then leaned back against it. "Whew," she said aloud, then stared at her hand in wonder. It had tingled at Charlie's touch. Tingled!

My, my, she thought, gazing at the pale skin, shades and shades lighter than Charlie's, and wondering if it continued to give off the heat she'd felt in that brief few moments of contact.

"My, oh, my," she said now, climbing the stairs to her bedroom for a quick shower before getting dressed. She had about twelve minutes to get ready, but she used only a little makeup, and her hair did what it wanted to do, whatever else she might intend for it to do, so it was never much trouble.

She paused halfway up the stairs when she realized her heart was pounding loudly and she needed to catch her breath. It wasn't the stair climbing that had made her heart race and her breathing quicken. No, it was that brief touch from Cowboy Charlie.

Or whatever his name was. For a moment she regretted sending him away. But at least he'd gone. Which was good, she assured herself, continuing her journey upstairs. Yes, much better...for all concerned.

She made it back down thirteen minutes later, which wasn't bad. After retrieving her purse from the hall table, she grabbed a ring of keys from a hook and pulled open the door.

No Charlie.

She admitted to a brief sense of disappointment. Not that she'd *expected* him to be waiting there, she told herself. Not that she'd *wanted* him to be waiting there.

No, that wasn't it. She'd done the right thing, been firm, set her boundaries, let him know that the water and coffee and cookies were all he could expect from her, and that she had a busy life to lead that didn't include his presence.

She sure had let him know. Good for her.

She closed the door, then used her key to double lock it. When she turned around again, she gasped.

There he was, standing there, big as life. It was as though he'd appeared out of thin air!

Charlie tipped his hat. "Didn't mean to scare you," he said, feeling awful as he took in Cassie's startled reaction. You should never sneak up on a body like that, and he sure hadn't meant to do that this time.

"Where...where did you come from?" she asked him, her hand on her throat.

"You said not to wait on the porch, so I was over there—" he angled his head to indicate the direction "—at the side of the house."

"Oh. Well, then," she said, and let out a deep sigh. He watched as the color returned to her face. "You took me literally then. You didn't just...materialize from...nowhere?"

"No, ma'am."

"Good," she said. "I really don't think my heart could take that." She seemed to gather herself together and walked purposefully down the two porch steps and onto the path leading to the street, saying, "Well, I'll be on my way then."

He followed. She stopped, turned to him again and offered her hand, just as she had done in the house. In the full morning sunlight, he could see tired lines around her eyes, and he had to resist the urge to run a thumb over them to smooth them away. She was too young to look so worn-out.

"You really can go now, Charlie," she said with a smile. "Thanks for brightening up my day. It was nice meeting you."

Again her hand was soft, and this time, when she tried to pull it away, he didn't let it go. "The feeling's mutual. It's just, you haven't told me yet what I'm supposed to do for you."

"Are we back to that?"

"Never left it."

She blew out a breath, and one of her bouncy brown curls lifted momentarily off her forehead then settled back into place. He sure did want to see how that healthy looking hair would feel between his fingers, sure did want to touch some more of her skin. But first he needed to get his assignment.

"Right. Fine," she said, looking from their still-joined hands and back into his gaze. His gut told him she was dismissing both his request and him.

"You can go to the bank," she said. "That's First Yatesboro Savings on Main Street. And get them to give me thirty more days on the mortgage. Okay? If you can do that, maybe I'll believe in Santa Claus. At least, maybe I'll believe in you." Gently she pried her hand out of his and walked away.

He watched her sashay off down the walkway and get into her small blue machine. *Car.* Unbidden, the word came to his head. He might have come from the Old West, but, for some reason, he now knew that was the name for the machine, same as he knew it ran on fuel made from oil pumped out of the ground.

He was getting this thing now, this transformation; clearly, he would have been granted all the knowledge he would need to function in Cassie's twenty-first-century world.

Now all he had to do was furnish a miracle.

Chapter Three

Frowning, Charlie watched Cassie drive away. Automobiles sure were wondrous things. Some of the newer characters in his world bragged about the inventions in "real" life, and he had to admit a car was convenient—though of course it couldn't beat Felicity.

So, go to a bank and deal with a mortgage, that was what he was supposed to do for Cassie, was it? Get her a thirty-day extension. Which meant she was short on money.

It was a classic scenario, the little widow woman with child, the wolf, or mortgage holder, at the door, waiting to pounce. It could almost be one of Cassie's stories. Starring him.

What would she have him do, if this were one of her stories? A scene flashed through his mind involving heading into the bank and pointing his six guns at whoever handled mortgages there....

No, he knew instinctively. They didn't do things

like that nowadays, he didn't think, not without serious consequences. And besides, like Felicity, his bullets hadn't made the trip through time and space, either.

Still, he had to take action, and better now than later. First, though, he removed his spurs. They jangled too much and slowed him down. No horse to ride, no spurs necessary.

He took both the spurs and the guns in their holster to the garage and left them there. Then, deep in thought, Charlie began to walk in the direction of the few tall buildings he could see in the distance. He figured those buildings would be the center of town. The business district, that was what it was called. The business district. He rolled the words over on his tongue. Formal sounding words, those.

He walked on paved sidewalks—another first for him—and passed small, modest houses similar to Cassie's. The lawns were so green, so even. And the houses were so close together, he marveled. You could look into each other's windows and see all kinds of private acts, he figured. Back home you could get shot for doing that. But not, he assumed, here. Maybe neighbors didn't look at neighbors? No, more than likely they did, but just pretended not to see.

Where did the folks here have room to grow their vegetables? he wondered. And how could you breathe with your neighbor so close?

First Yatesboro Savings, Cassie had said. He kept an eye out for the sign as he stopped at a cross street named Main. Funny, there was a Main Street back home. Did every town have a main street? It warmed him, this small connection. Maybe things weren't that different here, after all.

Small machines—cars—like Cassie's but with different shapes and colors, passed him by. No horses, though. He didn't see one, which made him kind of sad. Were there horses anymore in Cassie's world?

He was crossing Main to get to the other side, when he heard a loud screech and a man's voice yelling, "Hey, cowboy! Can't you see it's red?" The car was right close to him and the driver looked pretty mad.

Red? Charlie gazed around him, then up at the sky, and sure enough there was a box hanging in the middle of the street. It had three circles on it, and one of them was red. He watched as that color went out and the one at the bottom it turned green. Other folks joined him now crossing the road.

"Sorry," he called out to the irate driver. Another new rule to learn. Red meant you stopped and green meant you could go. And yellow must mean to pay attention, he told himself. This new way of thinking was slowly seeping in and part of it must come from Cassie's belief that he knew about modern life.

He began to notice the other folks now, probably because in this part of town there were a lot more of them. His gaze landed on a couple of women in real short skirts, their legs bare as a newborn, their hips swaying back and forth as they went. A right pleasant sight, Charlie thought with a smile. Did they work for the town madame he wondered, or were they what back home they'd call "independents"? He turned his gaze to the other side of the street; there were a lot of women dressed like those two, but a lot who weren't. Some wore pants, just like men, although they didn't look like men. No, sir.

Now he passed a row of stores, some of them with familiar words on the windows, like Druggist and Bar, others with funny names like Computer Closet and Beanie Babies' Barn. He didn't know what computers or Beanie Babies were, but he figured it went along with modern times, and if he needed to know about it, he would.

Up ahead a couple streets, it looked like the buildings just stopped. In the distance he could see a highway, fields, mountains rising tall into the sky. They looked a lot like his mountains, and Charlie experienced a sudden wave of yearning to be back home, back in his simple existence.

He shook himself out of that one, right quick. He had a job to do, a woman to help. A woman he liked very much, as a matter of fact, and who didn't exist back home. Not in any real sense, anyway.

Pausing, he looked around him. Yes, he decided, for a modern town, it was a pretty little place, no doubt about it.

And wouldn't you know it, he had stopped right in front of the sign he'd been looking for: First Yatesboro Savings. He removed his hat and scratched his head. Here it was, the job he was supposed to do. Get that mortgage extended, give Cassie a little time to earn more wages.

Or maybe *he* could do that for her. He would do more than buy her time, he'd come up with enough money to ease her burden. How, he didn't know, but it would come to him. Squaring his shoulders, Cowboy Charlie headed into the bank.

Cassie had several responsibilities at the dress shop. She helped customers, was backup for the cashier, straightened racks of clothing. But because she had an eye for color and fabric, her biggest responsibility was the window display. At the moment that was where she was, in the shop window, draping a paisley shawl over one of the mannequin's shoulders, when she happened to glance out on the street.

Charlie stood in front of the bank, studying it and scratching his head as he did. Good Lord, she thought with a smile, he's actually going to do it. Or try to, anyway.

What would happen? she wondered. Would he get anywhere? As she rearranged the vase of silk geraniums she'd set on the small table near the mannequin's hand, humming a little tune to herself all the while, she let her mind drift for a few moments.

She was surprised by the way Charlie's determination to help warmed her insides. It was a nice feeling, she realized, to have someone—wherever he came from—in her corner, taking her part. It had been such a long time. Most days she woke up with a hollow, *lonely* feeling, and something about Charlie's presence this morning, if she were honest with herself, had diminished that feeling, made her feel less alone.

And now, her champion—she chuckled as the word came into her head, but there it was—her knight in shining armor and a Stetson, was across the street, doing battle in her name. Fanciful image, she knew it, but that was the mental picture that formed when she thought about Charlie.

She hoped he wouldn't be disappointed if he didn't get anywhere with the bank. Charlie might be big and strong, but he hadn't yet met the loan officer in charge. When he did, he would find out what he was up against.

Cassie's hand stopped in midair. The loan manager, Ronald Moffit, was not exactly a warm, welcoming type; how would he react to Charlie? Suddenly she had a bad feeling about having issued her challenge. What if Charlie got thrown out? In fact, what if he made the whole situation worse? Uh-oh, she thought, coming down from daydreaming with a thump.

"Lorna," she called out, hopping down from the display window and into the shop, "I'm taking my break." Quickly, before anyone noticed that she'd only been on the job for a half hour, she pulled open the front door and, dodging traffic, made her way across the street.

"You're here on behalf of whom?"

Charlie shifted his weight as he stood before the desk he'd been directed to, the one belonging to the loan officer. He didn't care for the man or his attitude. First of all, he was not more than mid-thirties, but was dried-up looking, like he'd died a while back and no one had bothered to tell him. He spoke through his nose in a way that grated on Charlie's nerves. His skin was pasty white, and what he had hairwise was thinning.

Judging a man by his appearance wasn't a fair thing to do, and Charlie knew it. He kept it as pleasant sounding as he could when he asked, "Okay if I sit?"

"Why don't you tell me your business first."

He felt his jaw tighten. Moffit was the sneering type, just like those college fellas Charlie ran into back on the range. The kind who came out west for adventure and who figured as Charlie hadn't gone past grammar school and dealt with horses all day, they had to talk real slow and careful to him, just in case he was a little lacking in the brain department. Charlie didn't like being looked down on. It was most definitely one of those little character traits that set his temper on the boil.

Rein it in, he told himself. He was here to help Cassie. He would contain himself, if it was the last thing he did.

"I'm here on behalf of Miz Cassie Nevins," he said friendly-like.

"Oh yes, Mrs. Nevins." The man gave a superior sniff. "We own her home."

"That right? I thought you owned the mortgage."

With a condescending little smile, Moffit waved a hand. "Semantics. And is that the matter you've come to discuss?"

"Yes, that's why I'm here."

Moffit glanced at his watch. "I have an appointment in a couple of minutes."

He didn't invite Charlie to sit, which he knew was an insult. He shifted his weight from one boot to the other, careful to keep his hands relaxed at his side. They kept wanting to curl up into fists, and that might not look real neighborly.

He stared at the loan officer. In the jacket pocket of his three-piece suit a yellow handkerchief stuck out, its edges folded neatly. Yellow, Charlie figured, like the butt-ugly coward he was.

"I figured," Charlie said easily, "between the two of us, we could figure out the best way to help her keep that little house."

Moffit eyed him up and down, then sniffed again. "Do you have some sort of documentation, some letter, that allows you to speak for her? I can't believe you're her lawyer, although I suppose with Mrs. Nevins, anything is possible."

"What exactly to do you mean by that remark?" Charlie's fists curled automatically. The man was making some kind of disparaging comment about Cassie, and that was not something he'd stand still for.

"Charlie! There you are!" Charlie was taken by surprise as Cassie came up behind him and grabbed one of his clenched fists. Good thing, too. One fist had been about to find its way to the pointy, smug chin that belonged to Mr. Yellow Handkerchief.

"Good day, Mrs. Nevins," the loan officer said.

"Hello, Mr. Moffit." Cassie was being cheerful at the same time she was tugging at Charlie's hand, like she was trying to signal him in some way. "I see you've met Charlie," she went on brightly.

"He said he was here representing you."

"Well—" Her chuckle sounded as false to Charlie as a set of store bought teeth. "Um, yes, I suppose he is...in a way. He's my...good friend. An old acquaintance, you might say. And when he found out that money was a little tight and I was going to have trouble with this month's payment, he just thought he'd come here and see if there was anything we could do about it." She chuckled again. "Old friends, like I said."

My, Charlie thought, she did run on and on when she was nervous, and this Moffit fella made her downright fidgety.

Moffit frowned at her, then at Charlie, then back at her. He steepled his pale fingers on the desktop. "I'm afraid you've been late too often."

"Twice. And only three days each time."

"Nevertheless I can't see that we'll be able to make any accommodation. After all, you signed a contract for a line of credit—"

"No, my late husband did that, as I've explained, without my knowing it."

That smug smile again, a dismissive wave of his hand. "Yes, well it's the same thing, isn't it. Believe me, we'd rather not take back the house, it's not worth a lot to us, but rules are rules."

Charlie had about had enough of this man's bullying. "When's this money due?"

"Last month's was due six days ago, but is officially overdue on Friday. That's three days from now. If we don't have that payment plus the current one, plus a late penalty payment by—" he consulted a desk calendar "—next Tuesday, that's after the Fourth of July holiday, well, I'm afraid we'll be discussing foreclosure proceedings."

Charlie began to speak, but Cassie tugged at his hand again. "I understand," she said.

That old familiar sense of shame washed over Cassie. Oh, how she hated being in debt, hated owing anyone for anything. Her life with Teddy had been all about keeping one step ahead of creditors, and she was sick to death of it.

Right now all she wanted was to get out of the bank, away from Moffit, as fast as she could. Especially as Charlie had just banged his fist on the banker's desktop, startling her and making Moffit jump in his seat.

"You'll get your money, by God," he growled. "I give you my word on it!"

Moffit put a hand on his phone, as though about to

summon help. Cassie grabbed Charlie's arm and pulled at him. "Come on, Charlie. Thanks so much, Mr. Moffit, you've been so kind."

"Kind?" Charlie said heatedly. "Kind? Why, you mean little—"

"Charlie, please," she begged, "we need to go now."

It took all her strength to get him out of there, but finally they stood on the sidewalk under the bank awning. People passed by, going around them.

Cassie was heartsick, but Charlie was sputtering his indignation. "That lily-livered, skinny skunk! Why, I'd like to—"

She cut him off. "Oh, Charlie, how could you?"

"How could I what?" He turned his turquoise gaze on her, his eyes as intense, as angry, as a storm at sea.

At the expression on his face, she jumped back, dropping her grip on his arm. Who was this seething man? *Her* Charlie was a more gentle, reasonable man. The Charlie *she'd* written didn't have a quick-trigger temper, didn't seem on the verge of blowing his stack. She wasn't quite sure how to talk to this Charlie, not in his current state. In truth, his barely leashed rage frightened her.

He seemed to sense her fear because he took in a deep breath, let it out, then said more quietly, "Hey, Cassie, I didn't mean to take a piece of your hide that way." Looking down at his feet, he shuffled them for a moment, then raised his head and gazed at her. "Sorry," he said, this time with a small, crooked grin. "He set me off."

"Oh, Charlie," she said sadly, "you've done the

same thing to him. Now I don't have a chance of an extension."

"Did you have one before?"

"No, but I had hoped—"

Out of nowhere tears welled up, blurring her vision. Mortified, she turned away so he wouldn't see and walked a few steps into the nearby alleyway. There, in the relative shade, she let herself cry. Charlie had followed her, and now he grabbed her by the shoulders and pulled her into his embrace. A middle-aged female passerby glanced into the alleyway, stopped momentarily, then went on her way.

"There, there." Charlie patted her awkwardly. "It's okay darlin', really it is. It'll be okay."

At the first feel of his arms around her, Cassie tried to pull away. But then she changed her mind. How could she help it? He felt so good. So big, so strong, so steady. He smelled faintly of stables and warm sweat, a truly masculine smell. It was such a luxury to have a man's arms to bury herself in, such a lovely feeling to have a warm chest to cry on.

So she let herself do just that, for only a short while, she told herself. In between sobs she sniffled, tried to explain. "You don't understand."

He continued to rub her shoulders. "What don't I understand, darlin'?"

She raised her tear-stained face and looked at him. "I never cry. I'm embarrassed."

"But it's good for you to cry. It's what you gals have over us men—you can cry." His broad hand on the back of her head urged her once more into his embrace. "So cry away. I'm here."

"Oh, Charlie."

How sweet, how tender were his simple words.

They had the effect of making her tears come even faster and harder.

She didn't question why she trusted this newcomer in her life to such an extent that she could lower her guard around him, only knew that it was all right to do so. Soon she was letting all of it out, all the pain of being alone and terrified, of being consistently short of money, of feeling unloved and of not being held for such a very long time.

Lord, Lord, Lord, Charlie thought, one arm tight around Cassie's narrow shoulders, the other stroking her soft curls. Such a little thing, and she felt so good, so right, there in his arms. Heck, the top of her head didn't even make it to his chin.

He'd surely messed up with the bank manager—that weasel—but at least he could offer her comfort. But he was a man, and that meant he was having a hard time keeping it to mere comfort. Her small, shapely body felt warm and womanly in his arms, and he had to swallow down the urge to lower his hands so he could rub her back. Other parts of her too. Her front, her sides, her bottom. All of her, in fact, every inch.

This was not what he'd expected from his visit to the real world. A soft woman in his arms and all his body parts on alert, an urge to open up the back of his throat and howl at the moon.

When Cassie, her sobbing now turned into small sniffs, let out a feathery sigh and snuggled deeper into his embrace, he just couldn't help himself. His mouth found its way to her neck, and he got a whiff of that nice fresh powder smell of hers. He heard her quick intake of breath, and in the next moment she moved in even closer, if that was possible, squirming into him like a kitten looking for the crook of an arm. He'd wondered and now he knew—she liked him the same way he liked her, as a woman likes a man. That knowledge felt good and made their future all the more exciting.

Then, in an instant, it was over.

Cassie pulled away, head lowered, wiping tears away from under her lids. Then she gazed up at him, almost shy now. Her eyes, large and chocolate brown, seemed particularly huge with their slightly pink lower lids. Poor, sad little thing, he thought. Beautiful, cuddly, sad little thing.

"Charlie—" Her voice broke and she coughed. "I—uh—thanks for the shoulder. But I have to get back to work now." And like that she wheeled around and headed off across the street, dodging a car as she did.

He followed her, also making sure he didn't get in the way of one of those machines. "I feel real bad about this, Cassie," he told her fast-moving back. "My temper gets agoing there sometimes, and that man, that Moffit, well, he's what we call a bad 'un. It makes him feel good to make folks feel bad."

Cassie nodded. "Yes, Mr. Moffit has some issues with power."

"Huh?" They were across the road now.

"Never mind. I work there."

She pointed to a small shop that had a bright-green sign hanging outside, reading Lorna's Dress Shoppe. In the window there were three female forms, one wearing a real short dress, another a longer one and the third with nothing on at all. The sight of that last one made Charlie swallow. He knew it wasn't real, but it sure did look it, especially in the bosom area, where there were two small bumps at the tip of the larger ones.

Times most definitely had changed, he thought, thinking back to the cloth dummies Miz Jenkins used to cut her patterns on back home.

He didn't have time to dwell on that, however, as Cassie was pushing open the glass door to the shop, so he followed her inside. His ears were assaulted by the sound of strange music and the chatter of women. In the next moment, however, the ladies stopped their talk, and he was aware of several pairs of eyes watching him. A giggle broke the silence.

The minute she entered the store Cassie was aware of the change in the atmosphere. Of course, she thought, turning around. Charlie had followed her inside, the rooster entering the henhouse.

She stopped in her tracks and crossed her arms over her chest. "Have a good day, okay?" she said firmly, dismissing him.

But he didn't seem to have heard. Mouth open, Charlie gazed all around him, at the racks of clothing, the displays of necklaces and purses, and most definitely at the two other salesladies and several customers, all of whom seemed to have decided, at the same moment, that this male newcomer was the center of the universe.

"Charlie?"

"Hmm?"

He wasn't going to leave, Cassie thought. He seemed determined to follow her, like a friendly stray who has adopted a new owner without the owner acknowledging it.

"I have to work now," she said pointedly, "so you

need to go somewhere else." There. You couldn't say it any plainer.

His gaze, which had continued to peruse the small shop with both interest and amusement, returned to her. "Is there anything I can do to make myself useful?" He fingered the fringes of a suede jacket that was displayed at the head of a rack of other suede and leather jackets. "These are right nice duds."

"Hi, Cassie. Who's your friend?"

This smoky purr came from Jill, the fortyish, thrice-divorced, extremely top-heavy woman who ran the cash register. She sidled up next to Cassie and Charlie. "Are you in town for the rodeo, cowboy?"

Before Cassie could make introductions, Charlie's face lit up. "You're having a rodeo here in town?"

"We do it every year at the Fourth of July weekend," Jill said, easing closer to Charlie and batting her eyes at him. "It's been going on for over a hundred years, and we've only missed the years during both world wars. I always love it during rodeo week, because that's when all the *real* men come to town."

He seemed oblivious to her innuendo. "Well, now, whoop-de-doo, that's something we've got to see! What do you say, Cassie?"

"About what?"

"Why, us going to the rodeo. Trish will love it, all kids love a rodeo. Besides, I want to see if anything's changed. I was a fair hand at the bucking steer in my day, even if I do say so myself."

"You were?"

She was on the verge of saying she didn't remember writing about bucking steers, or anything remotely resembling a rodeo, when it came to her that sometime in the past hour or so, she had begun to think of

Charlie as who he actually claimed to be—her creation come to life.

Or at least she believed he believed he was who he said he was. Oh, God, maybe he was suffering from some kind of mental illness. He could be psychotic. Although he came off as pretty sane to her.

This was all horribly confusing. He seemed Charlie-like, but then he didn't. He spoke of being in a rodeo, but she'd never written a rodeo scene because she'd never had any interest in doing so. So how could Charlie—her Charlie—have done that?

Wait a minute. Why was she questioning his having been a participant in some ring with horses and bulls? Was she beginning to believe he really was her creation, come to life, standing there in front of her? And was she irritated because he seemed to have a life *beyond* the one she'd written for him?

But...if that were so, if Cowboy Charlie actually existed outside and apart from her imagination, then that meant he'd been born of two parents, had had a childhood, his own memories, his own experiences, things she had no knowledge of or control over.

Could it be? Was it possible to create something and have it assume its own life?

Like Frankenstein's monster?

No, not Charlie, not a monster, not in the least. He was a sweet, good, extremely masculine man who meant no one any harm.

Except that he had a temper. And loved rodeos.

What else didn't she know about him?

Not for the first time Cassie had the sense she was existing within the boundaries of an extended dream. Maybe she'd been in a really awful accident, and even now had one foot in the present and the other in the grave. The thought made her shudder. Was this a drug-induced fantasy while she was in a coma?

No! No! No! she told herself firmly. The whole direction of her thoughts was ludicrous and wasteful. It would stop, right now.

She gazed around at her co-workers. Had one of them been the one to set this up? She'd find out later. Right now she had a job to do.

"Cassie?" Charlie said, a puzzled look on his face.

"Huh?"

"I've been trying to get your attention, but you seemed to be off somewhere."

"Yes. Sorry." More disturbed than she wanted to admit, she shook herself, then met his gaze. "Yes? What were you saying?"

"I was asking about the rodeo," he explained patiently.

"I can't talk about that now. I have to get to work."

"All right, then," Charlie said slowly, as though he understood. "We'll talk about that later. Right now tell me what I can do to help you."

"There's nothing for you to do," she said firmly.

"Unless your friend, there, wouldn't mind a little heavy lifting?" Lorna Buchanan, the imposing, gray-haired, shop's owner, strode up to them, her customary several strands of beads bouncing against her ample bosom. "Larry called in sick and I've got some stuff that needs loading and unloading. You look like you're in pretty good shape, young man." She accompanied this observation with a pointed up-and-down perusal of his body.

"Well, ma'am," he preened, "I've never heard any complaints."

"I'm Lorna," she told him, as they shook hands.

"Charlie, ma'am. Right nice to meet you."

The gush of jealousy that swept over and through Cassie added to her jittery state of mind. *Hands off, he's mine,* she almost said, but bit her bottom lip to keep it from coming out.

Lorna, several times a grandmother, wasn't flirting with Charlie, for heaven's sake, not the way Jill had been. Easy, girl, Cassie chided herself silently, astonished at her strong need to claim him as her property. Astonished at all the strong emotions Charlie seemed to rouse in her.

Lorna took Cassie's silence as consent. "Good, then. Come with me to the stockroom, Charlie, and I'll show you what needs to be done."

Feeling helplessly swept up in something that was so out of her control that she hadn't one weapon in her arsenal to change it, Cassie watched as Charlie was led away to be put to work.

The man refused to go away. For the present at least, it seemed Cowboy Charlie—whoever he was in truth—was now a part of her life.

Whether she wanted it that way or not.

Chapter Four

The older lady, Lorna, reminded Charlie of Miz Jamison, the schoolteacher back home. Both of them were women who covered up marshmallow insides with porcupine outsides. In her gruff manner, Lorna quickly showed Charlie where things went and what she needed for him to do. He caught on just fine, happy for something to do while he waited for the answer as to how to help Cassie. As for Cassie, he said hello to her throughout the day, but she seemed too busy to stop and talk to him.

Or more than likely she was avoiding him.

Lorna advanced him some money so he could go to lunch, but when he went to find Cassie, she was just coming back from hers. As she passed him, she turned her gaze in another direction. Sure enough, she was mad at him, probably for two reasons.

First of all, he'd made the situation at the bank worse than it had been before he'd opened his yap.

And then he'd gone and put his hands on her. She

couldn't have mistaken his body's reaction to her, especially as close as they'd been standing. He hadn't forced himself on her or anything; no, she'd been willing, for sure. But still, she'd been in a fragile way, and he probably should have held himself apart a little more than he'd seemed able to.

It made Charlie feel sad that he'd upset Cassie. It was the last thing he wanted to do. He'd just have to make it all better. What would help would be to find a way to come up with money for her mortgage.

And he'd keep his hands to himself. Unless she didn't want him to. But if that was the case, she'd have to let him know—he'd let the lady set the pace. Which would be real difficult, truth to tell; ordinarily, Charlie was patient with women, but what he felt for Cassie didn't go with being patient.

Still, he would take it slow and easy, because all he wanted was for Cassie to trust him and to let him make her happy.

Meantime, there was a lot of work for Charlie to do. He put frilly blouses on hangers and racks and unloaded boxes and swept up pins and tags off the carpeted floor. This was sure a different world from Granger's General Store, which back home was where most of the ladies' clothing was sold. There were so many choices, he noted, so many colors and styles and fabrics. How could a body decide?

As he'd observed earlier, some of the garments were downright suggestive. They were see-through and low cut and real short, leaving nothing to a man's imagination. Still, the customers who came in to the shop and bought those clothes weren't ladies of the evening—far from it. No, they seemed to be regular folks, regular for Cassie's time, anyway.

While he worked he listened to their chatter and learned a whole lot. Many of them had full-time jobs, which was one of the big differences from back home. But there were just as many who spoke about their families. Each woman bragged on her child, positive that he or she was the brightest and smartest ever born. That hadn't changed at all, Charlie thought with a smile, and for that he felt glad.

At the end of the day Lorna was also nice enough to show him to a small bath in the rear, one that had a modern shower, which proved to be a pure delight. Hot and cold water came out of one spout and poured down all over a body. Plus, there seemed to be a never-ending supply. She found a razor for him, and after a little bit of adapting, he was able to give himself a passable shave.

When he informed Lorna that all he had to change into were the clothes on his back, she raised an eyebrow momentarily, but then found some duds for him. Work clothes, she said, which used to belong to her husband. The late Mr. Buchanan had obviously been as tall as Charlie, although he must have had fifty pounds on him, mostly in the gut area. Charlie managed to hold up the faded dungarees with his own belt, then donned a clean plaid shirt. Shoes were still a problem, though—he sure did have big feet—so he put his boots back on.

He caught up to Cassie as she was walking out the door.

"Hey, there, Cassie."

"Yes?" She turned, looked startled, as though her mind had been far away. "Oh, sorry, Charlie. I'm on my way to pick up Trish. She stays after school for two hours, but I have to be there by five or they get ticked off."

She hurried out the door, so he followed. She made her way to the small parking lot in the rear of the row of stores.

"Mind if I come along?" Charlie asked, following her.

She paused in the act of inserting the key into her blue car, then looked at him, her face scrunched up in a way that let him know she was pondering mighty important things.

"Well, Charlie, the truth is, yes, I do mind. I like you very much, but, somehow, ever since you turned up, I feel as though I'm supposed to be responsible for you, and I don't—"

He interrupted her. "You're not responsible for me, Cassie. It's the other way around, remember?"

She put her hands up, palms out, like she was warding off mud sprayed by a passing wagon. "Stop. Just stop. This has gone far enough." She licked her lips, then went on with determination. "I have a real life to lead, a real child to raise, real money to find within the next week, and I can't take any more of you. You're a—" she threw her hands in the air in a gesture of pure helplessness "—distraction!"

Leaning against the fender, Charlie pushed his hat back and scratched his head. Propping the heel of one boot against the tire, he nodded. He'd been right. "Yep. I figured you were angry with me."

"I am *not* angry with you," she said with some heat, then seemed to realize that she'd just contradicted herself. More quietly she said, "Oh, Charlie, I know you mean well. It's just that—" She shrugged.

"But I crossed the line. With Moffit."

"Yes, you did."

He tugged his hat back onto his head more firmly. "How about with you? Did I cross the line with you? Did our...touching each other cross the line?"

Startled by Charlie's directness, Cassie was about to say an unequivocal yes, but her innate honesty prevented her from doing that. "You did and you didn't. It was very sweet of you. I was in distress and you offered comfort. It felt good, for the moment, and I thank you for that. But—" she drew in a breath then blew it out "—there will be no more of that physical stuff. Not till I find out who you really are and where you really come from. If even then." Frowning, she added, "I mean, for all I know, you could be a serial killer."

"A what?"

"Never mind."

He pushed himself away from the rear bumper and stood facing her, his hands fisted at his sides. Uh-oh. Something she'd said had irked him again, but she stood her ground. Except that she had to crane her neck way back to meet his gaze.

"I'm no killer, Cassie." The look he gave her was intense, with just a bit of hurt mixed in. "I'll defend myself, if necessary, but I'm no killer."

As she'd suspected. She'd insulted him, and she hadn't intended to do that.

She put her hand on his arm. "Charlie. Listen I'm sorry, I know you're not evil, really I do. It's just that I'm so confused."

"About me?"

"No, no. Well, yes. Oh, I don't know." It was easier not to get into this. Exasperated, she opened the car door. "I have to get Trish."

"I know. That's why I wondered what you want me to do. She expects to see me when she gets home."

She glanced at him briefly, gave it a thought, then got into the car. "Then I guess she needs to learn that she doesn't always get what she wants."

"Oh." He nodded thoughtfully. "I see. All right, then. See you." He turned to go.

She paused in the middle of inserting her key into the ignition. "Where will you go?" It was out of her mouth before she could stop herself, and she cursed herself inwardly for blowing that nice, firm goodbye.

"I'll be fine." His attempt at a reassuring grin wasn't quite successful, and she saw that her dismissal had hurt him. "Miz Lorna said I can bunk down in the back of the shop."

"Oh. Good," was what she said, but what she was feeling was plain old irritation with her notoriously wary boss for being so generous. "Yes, fine. What about dinner?" Again the words sprang fully formed from her mouth, as though she had no vote in the matter at all.

"Dinner?" He leaned a hand on the open car door.

"You do eat, don't you?"

His grin was wide and genuine now. One lock of blond hair fell across his eyebrow as he replied, "Yes, ma'am. I have a powerful appetite."

His words, she was sure, referred to food. But still, "powerful appetite" stirred her, deep inside, evoking an image that raised a blush all over her body. Averting her face just a fraction, she asked, "Do you have money to get dinner?"

"Sure do." He pulled some bills out of his pocket.

"Miz Lorna was nice enough to advance me forty dollars."

Miz Lorna was being nicer than her nature usually allowed her to be.

"But you'll be eating alone." Again Cassie was unable to halt the words. Finally she just gave up trying. "Oh, come on over for dinner," she said, thoroughly disgusted with herself. "I made a big stew, and it's sitting in the refrigerator waiting for me to pop it in the microwave."

"The microwave? I'm not sure what that means."

"Come by in an hour or so and you'll see."

"Yes, ma'am," Charlie said happily.

Now why, she wondered again as she slammed the car door and started the engine, why in the world was she doing this? Charlie waved back as she took off, and she nodded grumpily back.

During the ten-minute drive to pick up Trish, Cassie kept asking herself the same question. Why hadn't she left well enough alone? Charlie had been perfectly happy to walk away; he had money for food and a place to stay. So why had she invited this man she was trying to get rid of to the house for dinner? What on earth had come over her?

It was the hug, she supposed. All day she hadn't been able to get that hug out of her mind. He was a wonderful, generous, *flawless* hugger. Most men wouldn't even come close to his proficiency. In Charlie's arms she'd felt so safe. It was as though she was, at long last, home.

And more than that. There had been a sense of ice melting, deep inside her, sensual, sexual feelings, the kind she hadn't experienced in such a long time. She missed the physical intimacy she'd had in her marriage. Not just the sex, but the closeness, the sense of *connection*.

Some quality in Charlie brought back that connectedness, with the added layer of making her feel both sexy and safe. It was a lethal combination—any man who offered all of these traits in one package might well be irresistible.

Guilt flooded her thoughts, for the moment at least. Teddy, bless him and his dreams, had never offered either safety or connection. She'd loved him dearly, but she had matured before he had, and he'd died before he had a chance to. For their entire relationship, he'd been a big child himself, with his mood swings, his vast plans and outrageous schemes that went nowhere. No, with Teddy she'd never really felt taken care of, never had that innate knowledge that if anything truly awful happened, he'd be able to shoulder the burden.

That was where Charlie was night-and-day different; despite his temper flare up with Moffit that afternoon, despite his stubbornness and conviction about his world, Cassie knew his character was as strong as his physique. He was a man a woman could lean on.

A warning light went off in her brain. There was danger in allowing herself to become dependent on anyone, but especially Charlie. Big-time danger.

She still didn't know who he really was. If one part of her believed his fiction-come-to-life story, the other, more pragmatic part of her still had some heavy doubts.

Which reminded her. The minute she got home, she was getting on the phone. Someone had set up this whole charade and, by heaven, Cassie was going to find out who.

The little girl answered the door with a big welcoming grin on her face. However, the grin faded to a disappointed pout the minute she saw him. "You aren't dressed in Cowboy Charlie clothes. Those pants are really baggy."

He lifted up the duffel bag in his right hand, keeping his left one behind him. "My clothes are in here and they're pretty grubby. I was hoping your mom would let me wash them here."

"Oh." The child took off toward the kitchen. "Mom!" she yelled. "Cowboy Charlie's here and he wants you to wash his clothes."

After easing the front door closed with his boot, he followed Trish into the kitchen. "Not exactly," he told Cassie. "If you'll point me to a basin and give me some soap, I can manage them myself."

"Hi," Cassie said, and before he could protest, she'd taken his bag, emptied its contents into a big white container in the corner, put some white stuff from a box on top, closed the lid and punched a bunch of buttons. "No problem," she told him. "They'll be done by the time you leave."

Her words were easy but she seemed preoccupied. A frown made a crease between her pretty eyes. "Thanks," he told her, then brought out his other hand from behind his back. "These are for you."

"Oh, Charlie," she said, surprise replacing the look of distraction on her face. "You shouldn't have." But she smiled, anyway, as she took the daisies and found a vase for them. "You shouldn't have," she said again, sniffing them, but he could tell she was pleased.

"Well, of course I should have. It's my way of thanking you for cooking dinner and for not biting my head off about the bank today and for finding me a job and for a whole lot more."

"I didn't—"

"You found Charlie a job?" the little girl asked, her gaze going from her mother to Charlie and back again, her face bright and eager.

"She sure did. I'm working where your momma works."

"Cool."

"I had nothing to do with that," Cassie said, "and you know it. It was all timing, that's all."

"Seems to me a lot of living is about timing. Which is why," he plowed on, "I want you to know that everything is going to work out just fine."

"And how do you know that?"

"Because I do, that's all. I just do."

She seemed to search his face for a few moments. Then, frowning again, said with a shrug, "Your faith is downright touching. Trish, wash up, honey. Dinner's almost ready."

He liked sitting in her kitchen. It was homey and warm. There were framed needlework scenes on the pale-yellow walls. The floor was wood, although some of the planks needed replacing. There were pots hanging over the stove. They were a dark-orange color, which he'd never seen before, but they looked sturdy.

The meal was sturdy, too. Big chunks of meat, potatoes and carrots swam in a thick, brown sauce. The only thing missing was salt, so he added some. But not too much because Cassie'd flavored the dish with some savory spices he wasn't familiar with.

The bread was fresh, and the butter tasted different from the sweet cream butter back home, but it was all right. He ate with gusto, so she pushed seconds on him, then thirds. Both mother and daughter watched him in amazement.

"It's like you've never eaten before," Cassie told him with a smile.

"Well, I have and I haven't, if you get my meaning."

That wiped away the smile, which was replaced by another searching look. All evening it was like she was studying him, looking for clues, trying to make sense of the situation and unable to make up her mind about him. A small cloud of confusion hovered over her gaze.

She still hadn't accepted him, the fact of his existence. The woman had to be the most skeptical person he'd ever met, for sure.

"It's good, real good, Cassie." He shoveled some more stew in, then decided he ought to stop. He wasn't full, but he didn't think he ought to make up for a lifetime of fictional eating in one sitting. But, oh, my, the real thing was so much better; no one had told him that.

Throughout the meal Trish peppered Charlie with questions, about Felicity and Marshall Tyler, the retired Civil War colonel who was his good friend. She wondered whatever had happened to Liza Mae, the little girl who had been so very sick. Charlie had ridden through a snowstorm to get medicine for her, and he'd arrived back just in time to save her life.

"She's just fine," Charlie told Trish. "Her momma

still has to rub her chest with wintergreen horse liniment when the winter comes, but she's growing up to be almost as pretty as you are."

Trish wrinkled her nose at the compliment, then asked, "How's Digger?"

"Well now, I'm afraid old Digger is gone."

"Gone?" Her sweet little face went from eager to sad in a second. "Digger's dead?" Her eyes filled with tears.

"Yep," Charlie said, wishing he could spare her, but knowing he couldn't. "He lived a good long life, did old Digger. Fourteen years is pretty ancient for a dog. One day he went to sleep and just didn't wake up, which is the best way for an animal to leave. We gave him a proper burial, Miz Chandler and me. After all, his barking saved the entire town from going up in flames."

The little girl nodded sadly, then wiped at her eyes with her napkin. "Still, I didn't know he died. Mom." She turned an accusing glare on Cassie. "You didn't tell me."

Cassie put her hand over her daughter's smaller one and squeezed it. "I didn't know." Then she looked over at Charlie and got that expression on her face again—confused and hopeful and mistrusting all at the same time.

"Oh," he said, feeling bad. "I'm sorry, then, to have to be the one to tell you both."

"How...how do you know about Digger?" As Cassie put it, it was not quite a question. "How could you know who he is...was?"

"Of course I know. It's from 'Charlie and the Daring Dog, Digger.'"

Trish piped in. "It's one of Mom's best stories, don't you think?"

"It's one of my favorites, too," he agreed.

"But I don't—"

Cassie didn't get to finish the sentence because the laundry timer went off, breaking the mood with its loud buzz. She had so many questions she wanted to ask, especially now.

Despite numerous phone calls to her girlfriends, she hadn't yet found anyone who claimed responsibility for this man masquerading as Cowboy Charlie. Or was it a masquerade? That doubting voice faded as, more and more, the evidence seemed to point to that which seemed impossible.

She rose and took his wet cowboy clothes out of the washer and started to put them in the dryer. She stopped in midmovement. "I hope these can take concentrated heat. Are they preshrunk, do you know?"

He shrugged. "I have no idea what that means."

She gazed at the clothing, then found a couple of wire hangers and hung them instead on a small hook by the back door. "Better not take any chances. They didn't exactly have wash-and-wear fabrics back then, did they?" She caught herself. There she went again, buying in to Charlie's story. How could she not?

"Just so long as they're dry by Friday night," he said.

Cassie began to clear the dinner plates. "What's Friday night?" When Charlie got up to help, she said, "No need."

He ignored her, picking up the rest of the dishes and carrying them over to the sink. "But I want to."

Side by side they stood there, her shoulder touching his upper arm. Even through their clothing, something happened to her skin as a result. His presence was impossible to ignore. It was like someone had plugged in a lamp and she was the conductor. Now all she could do was let that charge travel all through her, igniting her senses.

She risked a sideways glance at him, but he seemed to be concentrating on rinsing off the dishes.

"What's Friday night?" Trish asked, because Charlie hadn't answered her mother's question.

"The rodeo," he said. "It's the first night, the preview and parade, the poster said. And I was hoping we could all go. You and Trish and me."

Behind them, Trish bounced in her seat. "Oh, Mommy. Can we? Can we please?"

"Go to the rodeo?"

"Yes. You've never taken me before."

Cassie walked back to the table, cleared the butter, the bread basket. "I didn't know you were interested."

"I am! I am! All the kids' folks take them."

"It goes on all this weekend," Charlie said, taking the bread basket and butter dish out of her hands and setting them on the counter, "and lasts for three days."

"Can we, Mommy? Please?"

"We don't have the money—"

"As my guests," Charlie said pointedly, as though displeased she hadn't understood his invitation. "I'm working, aren't I? At least till the end of next week, Miz Lorna said, if I want to. The usual fella hurt his back."

Her initial impulse was to say no. Cassie had been off-kilter since Charlie had come to the door tonight, and now she couldn't decide how to react to him.

Here he was, not just inviting them to the rodeo, but dangling the temptation to believe in him in her face. And dangling that temptation not just in her face, but in Trish's too. Her daughter was so much more vulnerable, so much more prone to heartbreak than she was.

Still, there had been so little fun in both their lives lately. It was possible, she had to admit, that she was being rigid.

She allowed her face to relax into a smile. "I guess we're going to the rodeo on Friday."

Charlie grinned, and Trish reached up for a hug from her mother. "Yippee!" she said.

Cassie scooped her daughter up in her arms. She had no choice but to go along with the general merriment. Like it or not—and she suspected she liked it more than was good for her—Charlie was now a part of their lives.

What would happen? she wondered, then stopped asking herself that question, as well as the big one—where had he come from?

As Charlie had said, it would all work out. Now, whatever the outcome, she was along for the ride.

Chapter Five

Trish refused to go to bed unless Charlie accompanied Cassie to say good-night. When she was all tucked in, and had been thoroughly hugged by Cassie, she demanded a new Charlie story. This querulous tone grated somewhat, but Cassie understood that it was because of Charlie— Not only was her daughter still pumped up by her beloved hero's presence, but like most children she was getting away with as much as she could, trusting that Cassie wouldn't make a scene.

"I haven't come up with any new stories lately, Trish," she said firmly, heading for the door, "so we'll have to let it go tonight."

"How about if I tell you one, then?" Charlie said.

He perched on the edge of the bed and proceeded to enthrall her daughter with a simple story about a small town, one where a young orphan boy, Aaron, was discovered one day singing in the woods. He'd been doing this for years in private, but a wandering cowpoke heard him. His voice was a wonder and made people shiver to hear him.

The townspeople—who, for most of his life, had ignored the poor homeless boy, except to give him food once in a while or a job at harvest time—now went to work to raise the money to send Aaron all the way east to a big, big city there, to study with a singing expert. Aaron became a famous opera singer, and when he was on tour out west and was playing at a nearby town, some of the townsfolk rode all the way to see him. They came back filled with praises for the young man's gift, and right then and there set up a scholarship fund for any youngster who needed to study but didn't have the money.

Cassie stood at the foot of the bed, listening with mouth slightly agape. It was a charming story, although it had nothing to do with Cowboy Charlie rescuing anyone, had not much to do with Charlie at all, in fact, except as the tale teller. It was just a story, either one he'd made up, or—she gulped as she considered this—from his real, actual life.

Was that it, then? Was she finally allowing herself to believe in the existence, in her house, in this century, of Cowboy Charlie?

As he told his tale, he wove a spell around her daughter, for sure, Cassie observed. And when, at the end, Trish yawned sleepily and put her arms up for a hug, and Charlie gave her one and a gentle kiss on her cheek, the entire scene aroused conflicting emotions—warmth at the picture the two presented, offset by that same worry for her daughter Cassie had experienced at dinner.

Trish was getting attached to the man for sure. Teddy had died nearly two years ago, and the little girl was starved for a daddy. By accepting Charlie as part of their lives, Cassie couldn't avoid asking herself what she was getting herself and her daughter into here.

"One more hug from you, too, Mommy," Trish requested, and Cassie obliged, pleased that her baby still needed a mom's final bedtime reassurance.

Cassie followed Charlie out the door, closed it behind her, and when she turned back around, he was there. Just there, standing very close to her, looking down on her with a gentle smile. "She's a good one," he said.

Cassie shrugged modestly. "I don't have any other kids to compare her to, but I think she's pretty special."

"So's her momma."

They met each other's gaze and for a brief moment Cassie sensed that an unspoken message passed between them, one that reverberated in all of her nerve endings. There was so much in that one look—a shared pride in the little girl, approval of her lively personality and good health, and that always deeply felt prayer that she be spared any more heartache. To lose a father at such a young age was more than a child should have to put up with.

"Want some coffee?" she asked him, breaking the moment.

"In a little bit. First, may I see one of them?"

"One of what?"

"Your Cowboy Charlie stories. It's funny. I live them, but I'd sure like to see how they look written down."

"All right."

He followed her to the small alcove that served as

her office and where several brightly colored folders lay stacked on a bookshelf. "There they are," she said, pointing. "Take your pick."

He chose one with a red cover and thumbed through it. Nervous about his reaction, Cassie shuffled some papers on her desk while he read, sneaking occasional peeks at his face for reactions. What she saw were grins of pure delight, and his approval filled her with a glow that made her feel as though she could float.

As he walked over to her, Charlie shook his head with amazement. "Well, ma'am, not only can you write, but you sure can draw. Look at that." Chuckling, he pointed to a page.

It was a drawing of Charlie, leaning against a fence post, an expression of distaste on his handsome face.

"That's when I tasted the loco weed, and my insides protested."

"Yes."

Perching a hip on the edge of her desk, he flicked through a few more pages. "I sure do admire the way you can spin a yarn."

"So can you. The one about Aaron, it was touching."

"That wasn't a yarn, that happened."

She wanted to follow up on that comment, but Charlie was already pointing to another picture and shaking his head in amazement. "You are one talented lady."

She nodded her thanks, moved by the compliments to blush slightly.

"And here's where I was so angry at Chet Manson, for making fun of that poor simpleminded boy."

"You took care of Chet, didn't you."

"Well, it only seemed like justice to take him far out of town and let him walk back. Gave him a little time to think about his sins." His mischievous grin made her heart turned over.

"You're a good man, aren't you, Charlie?" she said softly.

"You ought to know," he said with a wink. "You made me what I am today."

Had she? Was it all true then, and was she ready to surrender to that reality, however bizarre it might be?

"Read away," she said, needing to think this through one last time. "I'm going down to make the coffee."

It has to be true, Cassie thought as she slowly descended the stairs. After her unsuccessful search for the practical joker, after all the discussion at dinner with his intimate knowledge of the details of the stories, she finally was getting it. Somehow the man reading through her stories really was the hero of those stories. Cowboy Charlie.

Had she stepped into another dimension, a Rod Serling *Twilight Zone* world? No, everything else in her life seemed pretty normal; it was just this one area. She could almost see her long-dead Grandma O'Toole nodding in approval. "See, child?" she would have told Cassie. "If there's no rational explanation, then just believe anyway. Go along, see where it leads. Not everything is visible to the naked eye."

She might as well surrender. Fighting it, denying it, poo-pooing it hadn't gotten Cassie anywhere. Besides, she liked that Charlie was real, instead of being some paid impostor, liked being next to him, smelling him, feeling the heat off his body, a body that awakened her senses in a fierce way. She was attracted to him. She wouldn't feel that way about a con artist or an actor. No, Charlie was real, end of discussion.

She didn't know where this would lead or what the next step was, but the river of life was flowing and she was a part of it, so she figured she might just hang on to whatever lifeboat Charlie represented and go along for the ride.

Her decision made, as she entered her kitchen a lovely sensation of peace filled Cassie's insides for the first time since Charlie had knocked on her front door—was it just last night? It felt a lot longer than that, years.

"I still can't stand that varmint Pete Plimpton," Charlie said, striding into her kitchen a few minutes later and planted himself next to Cassie at the kitchen counter. "He riles me up every time I think about him."

"That's because he's the only competition you have with all the ladies."

"Competition?" He snorted his disdain. "That time he tried to kiss Sue Ellen Logan? She slapped him silly. No woman's ever done that to me."

"If you'd tried to kiss Sue Ellen," Cassie said dryly, as she watched the final drops of coffee descend into the pot, "maybe she would have slapped you, too."

"Oh, I tried. And she sure didn't slap me."

Startled, she turned her head to look up at him. "When?"

He touched the tip of her nose with his finger. "Never you mind. We keep those little details for the grown-ups. They're not in your stories, because they're not for little ears to read about."

She felt a blush creep up over her face. "Charlie, you're embarrassing me."

"But you look so cute when you're embarrassed."

Suppressing a giggle, she turned to face him directly, her arms crossed over her chest with indignation. "Don't call me cute. And why did you kiss Sue Ellen? She's engaged to Donald McWhirter of the McWhirter Ranch. Isn't she?" she finished weakly, feeling another giggle forming in her throat.

"Nope. He was a no-gooder. She got rid of him, right after you ended the story. That's when I kissed her."

"I am so confused."

And jealous, too, she added silently. How dare Charlie kiss Sue Ellen Logan? But she kept those thoughts to herself, only sighed. "This is all so new to me. I mean, I never thought you had a life, I mean a real life, outside of the one I wrote for you."

"Well, ma'am—" his grin was all white teeth and lively turquoise eyes with laugh lines radiating out from the edges "—I'm here to tell you, I have quite a real life. No complaints at all."

In the next moment, as though a switch had been turned off, the gaiety left his eyes and his face took on a sober expression. "Except one."

"What is it?"

He cupped her cheeks with his hands, cradling her face. "Where I live," he said quietly, "you aren't there."

When she laid her hands on top of his, he angled her face upward. The kiss, when it came, felt quite real. There was no fantasy here. The slightly rough texture of his calloused hands on her cheeks, the touch of his mouth with its soft-yet-firm, knowing lips, these combined to create an impression of heightened awareness, a tingling sensation all over. Her senses were on fire.

She opened her mouth to allow his tongue inside. As though he'd been waiting for this signal, his hands left her cheeks and wrapped around her body, pulling her close. How very strong he was, Cassie thought through a mist of sensation unlike any she could ever remember. Hard and lean. The enormous strength of him was there in every sinew, muscle.

There was that other quality, too, that assuredness, the take-charge, you-can-lean-on-me-ness of him, and she had no other option than to melt against his warm, hard body, to feel herself yielding, trying to become part of him, dissolving into him.

Connecting…at last.

A loud groan interrupted the moment, and Cassie realized it came from her throat. The sound had the effect of snapping her back to the present. Ducking out of the kiss, she eased away from Charlie and stepped back, leaning against the tile counter. She couldn't help touching her mouth with her fingers, to see if they burned as hot as they felt.

Charlie remained right where she'd left him; the expression on his face was dazed and disoriented, just the way she felt and probably looked to him. As they had in the hallway upstairs, they stared at each other for a long moment, not speaking, their eyes telling all they needed to know. There was heat there and wonder. And just a little fear.

On a less emotional level, she couldn't help noticing the evidence of his desire for her—the zipper area of his way-too-big pair of pants bulged rather obviously.

It was Charlie who broke the silence. "Well, Cassie," he said with a rueful grin, one hand braced on the counter edge near him. "Well."

His understatement almost made her laugh. "Well, yourself."

"Did that just happen, or did I imagine the whole thing?"

She bit her bottom lip before she spoke. She was still reeling, but she made herself focus. Not five minutes ago she'd finally accepted the fact of him. To jump into a physical relationship so quickly seemed unwise, even as her body remained on sexual alert. "I think," she said slowly, "we'd better assume you imagined it."

His frown let her know he didn't care for her answer. But then he nodded. "Right. What you're saying is I better get going."

"Yes, but not till after you've had your coffee."

"I think I'll take a rain check on the coffee."

"Where will you stay?"

"In the back of the shop."

"Oh, that's right." In the afterglow of the kiss, Cassie still felt a little drugged, a little slow on the uptake, like she was in a waking dream. "But how will you get in?"

"She gave me a key."

"A key?" Her eyebrows shot up. Would wonders ever cease? "Lorna is not like that, you know, not easily trusting of, well, of anyone. You certainly have earned her trust."

He grinned. "That's me. Mr. Trustworthy. I intend to earn yours, too. I haven't forgotten that I'm here to rescue you."

She felt her back stiffen at this pronouncement.

Something about the word, or maybe the casually male way he said it, irritated her. "I've been doing okay, you know. I could always use a little support, maybe, but I don't think I need rescuing."

His eyes narrowed in a momentary look of assessment. "All right, then," he said with another small grin. "How about we put it this way? I'm here to offer an arm to hold, a shoulder to lean on, a little help. If you need it, of course."

She had to smile. He really was a charmer, although not in a calculated way. Charlie's nature was naturally giving. He was an anomaly in this day and age of self-centered people so busy getting somewhere they hardly ever stopped to pay attention.

But then again, he wasn't of this day and age. He was from a time when, as the expression went, men were men and women were women.

Whatever that meant. And if such a time had actually existed.

Her fictional Charlie lived in the late nineteenth century, in an area of plains, mountains and small towns that could have been located anywhere in Montana, Wyoming, Nevada, Colorado, New Mexico, Arizona or Idaho. The setting was purposefully vague, based on mythology and her own bedtime stories. Her father, who had been raised on fifties TV shows with heroes like Roy Rogers and Gene Autry, the Lone Ranger and Hopalong Cassidy, had brought this world to life for Cassie. The memories of those bedtime stories were still some of the best of her childhood.

"Sure," Cassie said to Charlie. "A little help sounds about right. Come, I'll walk you out."

At the door he put his hand on the knob, paused,

then turned to face her. His brows were knit, his mouth turned down.

She put her hand on his arm. "What, Charlie?" When he didn't respond, she said it again. "What is it? You're scaring me."

"I just remembered."

"What?"

"After I rescue you—I mean, help you— Oh, hell, whatever you want to call it. The thing is, I'm on a mission. There's a purpose to me being here."

"Yes?"

"And when that's done, when you're all saved, or rescued or whatever, then—" He stopped, left the sentence unfinished.

"Then what?" she prompted, her fear growing stronger now.

"Then...I think...I leave."

"You what?"

Frowning, he nodded slowly, looking deeply somewhere inside. "I'm remembering now, some of the tales they tell around the campfire back home. That's the way it works. After my task is completed, I have to leave. I have to go back. Home. Those are the rules."

Her breath stopped, as though someone had slammed a fist into her gut. "Oh, no."

In the silence that followed, his sad gaze roamed her face. "But, you see, what I'm starting to realize—" Again, lost in some internal thought, he left the sentence unfinished.

"What are you starting to realize?" she prompted.

He met her gaze with his own now. The lovely eyes were sad, filled with deep pain. "That I might not want to go back."

And I might not want you to, she almost said out loud, but not quite.

No, she wanted to say. *No.*

She pulled open the door and stood back. "Let's deal with that when the time comes, okay?"

He gazed at her briefly, then nodded. "You're right. Let's not think about that now. Let's just say good-night."

He leaned over, his face coming toward hers, for a kiss. Cassie put her fingertips on his mouth to stop him. "If you're going to leave soon, I think we'd better not, um, get physical."

"Not even a kiss?"

"I have a child," she began, and what she wanted to add was, *I also have a heart that is already on the way to being broken.* But better not. Why let him know how much he affected her? Why start something that had no chance of a happy ending?

"All right," he said. "See you tomorrow."

As she watched him walk down the pathway to the street, her mind struggled with the new information Charlie had relayed. The final wrinkle in the fairy tale. There always had to be rules. You find the ruby slippers and the witch dies, you return home before midnight or everything reverts, you say the magic name and you get to marry the prince.

This one was a new one on her, although it had the feel of a classic. The prince does his good deed and then he disappears.

Until what? Was there a magic kiss that brought him back?

Now she knew she had to be nuts, to be asking questions, reasonable questions, about an unreasonable situation. It was too much to take in, she told herself. Time for bed.

Still, one thing was clear: in the deepest recesses of her mind, Cassie now believed everything Charlie said. He was who he claimed he was—the character she had created out of the chaos in her imagination, come to life under extraordinary circumstances—if only for a brief time.

But even her acceptance of this didn't mean she didn't want some explanation. On her lunch hour the next day, she decided to stop in at her optometrist's. He was situated two blocks away in a small shop whose window display featured a pair of huge eyeglasses.

When she entered, a small bell went off. Dr. Slater, tall and bald, was behind the counter, polishing some lenses. Upon seeing her he smiled. "Hello, Cassie. How are those reading glasses working out?"

"They're just great." She looked around, but there were no other customers at the moment. She was in luck. "The headaches went away, just like you said."

"Good. They'll do fine, so long as you don't mind what they look like." He chuckled. "They sure were unusual looking, weren't they?"

"That's what I wanted to ask you about. You said they were an extra pair that came in a regular shipment. Where did they come from?"

"Well now, let me see." He opened a small brown drawer, just one of a tall bank of drawers, like an old-fashioned card catalog, thumbed through and pulled out a white card. He read it, then said, "The whole shipment came from Samuel Miller Associates, a wholesaler I use in Montebello, California. Been using them for years." He removed a paper clip from the card and unfolded a piece of rainbow-striped note paper. "This was wrapped around your pair."

"May I see that?"

He handed it to her. The colorful piece of paper was hand-lettered in an old-fashioned script, which read "Fashioned by Irma of Venice, California." No phone number, no address, no Web page. Nothing more.

"Do you have a phone number for this Irma?"

"Nope. Just the note."

He was nice enough to give her the phone number of his distributor, and later, when she returned to work, she went into Lorna's small back office and called them. They had no idea about an extra pair of glasses in a shipment, were adamant, in fact, that there couldn't have been anything extra in a shipment because their quality control people checked everything twice. They had never heard of this Irma, and by the time the phone call was over, sounded a little irritated with Cassie.

Next she called California information, but there was no listing in either the business or residence lists for anyone with the single name of Irma. As Cassie had no last name to go on, she was at a dead end in her quest to find out about the magic glasses.

If, indeed, that was what they were.

But it was all quite mysterious and lent credence to the whole magic theory. The sudden appearance—a gift from Dr. Slater—of an outlandish-looking, untraceable...*thing* that, when she rubbed it and made a wish, that wish was granted. It all fit.

"Huh," she said out loud, to no one in particular. She was still amazed that she was buying this whole thing. However, she thought with a grin, the truth was out. At the ripe old age of twenty-eight, Cassie Nevins, born O'Toole, had finally begun to believe in magic. And, interestingly enough, it felt good to have another reality to than hers face. Whoever this Irma was, she thought, well, bless her.

Pawing through her purse, she found the glasses, pulled them out of their case and stared at them. Ordinary. Except for the hideous color and shape, of course.

I wonder what would happen if I tested them again?

Not a bad idea. What had she been doing when she wished the other night? She couldn't really remember, but after her wish, Charlie had appeared at her door almost instantly. Instinctively she began to rub them, all over, like the genie-in-the-bottle story. Closing her eyes, she wished for—what? What would be the right thing to wish for? Money? No, that sounded selfish, somehow. World peace? Too big. Something small, something reasonable, attainable.

"There you are."

Cassie's eyes popped open to see Charlie in the doorway of the small office. Embarrassed, she set the glasses on the desk behind her purse.

"Hi," she said casually. She'd been civil to him all that morning whenever they'd run into each other, but that had been it. She didn't want any gossip getting around about the two of them, didn't want to pin any kind of hope on him, and didn't want to have her heart broken when—and if—he left.

"What are you doing, Cassie?"

"Nothing much." She frowned at her untruth, and brought the glasses out for him to see. "I'm testing these. I'm trying to think of something to wish for."

"I sure could use some lunch."

"You want me to wish for your lunch?"

"Nope," he replied with a grin, "I wondered if you'd like to go out with me?"

"I just took my lunch hour. I went to the doc to find out about these glasses."

"And what did you find out?"

"Nothing. Not a thing. They were sent by some untraceable lady in Venice. The Venice in California, not in Italy."

"She's probably a witch," he said matter-of-factly.

"A witch?" Dear Lord, the ease with which he offered that explanation jarred her. "I'm buying all this, about you coming here and all, but do I have to believe in witches, too?"

He shrugged. "Only if you want to."

"Okay, that's it. Let's go for it." She rubbed the frames all over and chanted. "I wish to know all about Irma of Venice, I wish to know all about Irma of Venice."

She waited. Nothing. No phone ringing with information. No magic smoke and a message from above. Nothing. Once again she rubbed the glasses, while Charlie propped a hip on the edge of the desk and waited.

"In the next five minutes," she intoned, her eyes closed now, "tell me all about Irma of Venice, California."

She waited some more.

"Day after tomorrow," Charlie said.

Startled, she opened her eyes. "What?"

"The rodeo. Friday night."

"Oh, right, yes. Trish is very excited."

"I am, too."

She rubbed the glasses, chanted again. The grandfather clock in the corner of Lorna's office had the loudest tick.

"That was a real good meal last night," Charlie said. "That stew. You truly know how to cook."

"Thanks, but it's easy. You just throw stuff in a crock pot."

"So they still have those."

"Yes, but they're electric now."

More seconds ticked by; they had to be near the end of her five minutes.

"What was that?" Cassie said, brought out of her concentration by a rumbling noise.

"My stomach, I'm afraid. I have a powerful appetite. A couple of hamburgers and French fries oughta do it."

"I see you've found the Burger Barn."

"Yes, ma'am," he said with enthusiasm. "That's powerful good stuff."

Cassie glanced at the grandfather clock. "Okay, that's it. The five minutes are up, and my wish hasn't been granted."

"That's because it only works once."

"What?"

"The magic. One wish, that's all you get."

She put her hands on her hips and glared at him. "Why didn't you tell me, before I began all this mumbo-jumbo?"

"Just found out myself."

"And just how did you come by that information?"

Shrugging, he said, "I just knew. It seems to happen that way." He stood up. "Anyhow, I'm off.

Gonna try my hand on those slot machines at the market. They sure are fun."

"To a point," Cassie said. Teddy had found them way too much fun, she remembered. She wasn't fond of gambling, but when you lived in a state where it was legal, you got used to it.

"Can I bring anything back for you?" Charlie asked.

"A sandwich." She took some money from her purse and offered it him.

"Put that away," he said. "In fact—" He pulled some bills out of his pocket and handed them to her. "This is for you."

"What's this?"

"Thirty dollars. It's not much, but at least it's part of the money you need."

"I can't accept this."

"Sure you can. It's why I'm here, right? To help with the mortgage."

Oh, Lord, she thought. What a sweet man. And what a sweet, silly gesture. Her eyes filled with completely unexpected tears. Embarrassed by the depth of her emotion, Cassie averted her gaze, busied herself putting the money back in her purse while she scolded him.

"Charlie, you haven't come from some far-off, other dimension place so that you can earn money taking dresses out of boxes and putting them on hangers and then give that money to me. That's not how it works."

"Really? How do you know?"

"I just do. It's...not dramatic enough."

"Oh, well. I'm new at this sort of thing."

She snapped her purse shut and looked up at him.

"So am I, for heaven's sake. Oh, just go, have lunch, please, just leave me alone." With that, she took herself off to the bathroom, effectively shutting down the discussion.

After a moment or two, when she heard Charlie's boots walking away, she returned to the office and sat down, her head in her hands. She felt totally disoriented, as though she was losing her bearings.

Cassie was beginning to fall in love with a man she'd met a day and a half ago, a man who didn't exist, except in her imagination, and in the flesh for a very short time.

Her solid belief system of "if you can't see it it isn't there" had been shattered.

The ugly reading glasses only worked one time.

She was on the verge of losing her house unless there was a miracle.

The embodiment of that miracle had just offered her thirty dollars on his way to the Burger Barn.

As an extra added attraction, if that miracle did occur, wherein Charlie actually saved the day, he would leave, and then she would be alone again, to raise her child and dream her dreams.

But with a new loss on top of the old one and a greater emptiness than before.

Chapter Six

Lorna closed up shop at 3:00 p.m. on Friday, so everyone could go to the opening parade and carnival. Cassie took Charlie for his first ride in a car, which felt kind of strange to him but also made him want to learn how to do it. Together they picked up Trish at school, and by late afternoon they were on the grounds of the annual event. Charlie couldn't believe his eyes—he'd never seen so many folks gathered in one place before. The noise, the bright colors, the smells—they overwhelmed his senses.

They also made him feel like a young boy again. There was a spinning-around ride and a Ferris wheel, and he got to take Trish on those because Cassie said her stomach couldn't handle them. His stomach didn't seem to suffer at all. Even though he tasted everything as they walked around, it all stayed down just fine. There was cotton candy and popcorn and wieners, which he had back home on special fair days—the modern versions didn't taste as good. There was also saltwater taffy and snow cones, both new to him, but were they ever delicious!

The local 4-H club sponsored a petting zoo, and he and Cassie smiled broadly while Trish cuddled a lamb and stroked a baby goat and fussed over fuzzy little chicks.

They found seats high in the bleachers for the opening ceremonies, which was mostly just a small parade around the arena, pretty girls in bathing suits and cowboy hats sitting on fine-looking horses and waving American flags. By now Charlie was used to scantily dressed women and the fact that the flag had more stars now than it did back home. He wasn't sure how he felt about all this change, but it didn't much matter because it was all happening so fast his brain could barely keep up with his eyesight. Besides, everything changed, all the time, and there wasn't much a body could do about it.

At least the events in the rodeo were the same as back home, and that pleased him. Tonight's contests were for kids and teenagers. Team calf roping was where a calf was released from a chute and two young folks on horseback had to lasso it and tie three legs, and do this as fast as they could. In barrel racing, barrels were set at either end of the arena and teenage girls on horses raced from one end to the other, around the barrels as close as they could without touching them.

Everyone had a good laugh at the mule "races," if you could call them that. Several mules were let out into the center of the corral, and young boys and girls rushed to mount them bareback and ride them to the finish line. Trouble was, the mules had other ideas, like stepping aside just as a rider was swinging up, causing that rider to land on his own posterior instead of the mule's back. If he did get to mount the mule, there was no getting the critter to move, or it moved in the wrong direction.

The audience chuckled and chortled, which felt so good, Charlie thought, beaming happily as Cassie and Trish wiped tears of laughter from their eyes.

Finally the riders who would be competing over the next few days paraded around the arena. As each one came out, Charlie did a running commentary for his two lady friends, explaining the moves, naming the horse breed, commenting on the gait or the way the rider sat his mount.

Cassie didn't remember ever having more fun and wondered how she'd managed to miss this event all these years. But it wasn't the event that was making it fun, she had to admit, it was Charlie and his boyish enthusiasm. She took notes in her head, as even now a story was forming. "Cowboy Charlie and the Rodeo." Maybe she'd come up with some crooked types who were hurting the animals or trying to get one of the riders to throw an event. Charlie, of course, would unmask the bad guys and save the day.

Trish sat between them, which seemed a safe thing to Cassie. She and Charlie appeared to have come to an unspoken agreement to keep their distance. He'd been over for dinner again last night, again had been attentive to Trish, had helped Cassie put her to bed, then had left, tipping his hat as he did. There was a sadness on his face when he walked away, and it matched the sadness in her heart. But she believed him when he told her he'd be leaving after he'd accomplished his mission, and she didn't want to mourn anyone again.

However...

Now her imagination took a left turn, from composing a new story to "what-if?" land. What if he didn't leave? Hmm. What if he stayed around? To do that, of course, he would have to fail at rescuing her. Great, then she'd lose the house and they'd have nowhere to live and she'd be stuck with a stock boy.

Not that there was anything wrong with stock boys, she thought with a chuckle, if you were eighteen and starting out.

"Whoo-ee!" Charlie whooped. "Did you see that one, Cassie?"

She shook her head; she'd been off in her head again, not paying attention. "What?"

He pointed to the ring. "Him. He's a good one, that cowboy. Roland Hawkins, they said his name was. He's the best I've seen in some time. Stayed on that roan for quite a while. See that, Trish?"

But Trish had fallen asleep. Against Charlie's arm. Her round child's face still had pink residue from the cotton candy, and there was mustard on her T-shirt. Cassie's heart turned over at the sight of the large man and the sleeping child. When she looked at Charlie, she knew for certain that he was considering the same what-if she was.

Charlie had to swallow down a real big emotion as he gazed into Cassie's eyes. He'd never had this feeling before, this...longing. He wanted to be this little girl's daddy and Cassie's husband. Tonight would be a typical family outing for them, and when it was over, the three of them would go home to their little house, turn out the lights and go to sleep. No, first he and Cassie would read to Trish. Then, alone, they'd talk over the day, then sleep.

No, he amended again, not sleep, not him and Cassie. They would show each other what they were feeling, touch each other, love each other.

He forced himself to cut off the fantasy. *That isn't going to happen, cowboy,* he told himself firmly. There was no cozy little family picture in his future. His existence was temporary. There were a lot of wide-open spaces between woolgathering about what could be, and what was fated to be. And there was no way he could see himself crossing those spaces.

He looked down at the child, smoothed some hair out of her face and sighed. You didn't fight what was in the cards; you didn't break the rules. Not these rules.

This time when he met Cassie's gaze he tried to smile at her, and she tried to smile back. But neither of them could quite pull it off. Yeah, she'd been thinking the same thing. And it was hurtful for her, too.

"Time to go?" he asked.

"Yes. It's way past her bedtime."

Besides, he'd had enough. From what he'd seen, they were real good, these rodeo riders, real good, probably as good as he was.

As they walked toward Cassie's car, Charlie carrying Trish and Cassie by his side, his mind was taken up with dreaming again, thinking about how he could earn a living, that is, if he were allowed for some reason to stay here, and if, as he believed, Cassie felt the same way toward him as he did toward her. No harm just thinking, was there?

Maybe he could be a rodeo rider. No, he corrected himself immediately. That was no life for a family man—it was nomadic and seasonal and most of them were hard drinkers and lonely.

But what did he know but horses and roundups and a little animal doctoring and watching the sun lower behind the mountains? For where he lived he had skills enough, money enough, a decent enough life…as a man alone. As a family man, what was he fit to do?

On Saturday night Cassie sat hunched over her kitchen table, sketching the picture she'd had in her head all day. It was Charlie, perched on a boulder in the middle of the desert, one leg stretched out in front of him, the other bent at the knee. He rested his elbow on that knee, his hand dangling between his legs, and stared off in the distance, a dreamy expression on his face. His hat partially shaded his face, bringing out the sharp angles of his cheekbones.

At the moment she was irritated with herself; she couldn't seem to get the mouth right, the shape of the bottom lip….

A knock at the door made her jump. She glanced at her watch. It was nine-thirty, and she wasn't expecting anyone. Clutching her robe around her, she went to the front door. "Who is it?"

"It's me, Charlie."

She hadn't seen or heard from him all day, and her heart lifted as she opened the door. "Hi. Come in."

"I bought this for Trish." As he stepped inside he showed her a small stuffed animal, a mule with one ear up and the other bent. It was adorable.

She took it and stroked the soft fur. "Oh, Charlie, you shouldn't spend your money on presents for her."

He looked down, shuffling his feet. "Well you won't take it, and it isn't doing me any good."

Charlie was not his usual upbeat self, she could see, so she immediately forgot her sketch. Hugging the toy to her chest, she said, "Trish isn't here."

"She isn't?"

"No, she's at Lisa Thomas's house, a pajama party. Several little girls get in their pj's and stay up way too late and eat too much and try to scare each other with ghost stories. It's a rite of passage."

He nodded, then gazed down at his boots again. He seemed distracted. This was not the Charlie she was used to, easy-going, positive. Not self-doubting, not complicated. Tonight he was all too human, and the urge to comfort him was strong.

"Come have some coffee," Cassie said, walking away.

"I don't mean to intrude." He followed her.

"You're not. I need a break."

In the kitchen she turned her pad over so Charlie couldn't see what she was drawing, then poured coffee into cups from a full coffeemaker. He stood behind her, not crowding her, just there. As was usual when they were in close proximity, she felt his presence like heat emanating from a radiator and seeping into her body. He presented a powerful temptation, and for a moment she allowed herself the fantasy of sleeping with him.

Trish was gone overnight, so that wasn't a problem. Why couldn't she give herself the gift of one night with this man? She craved him, after all. Why not give in to that craving?

Because it might feel good for one night, but would leave her desolate for many nights afterward.

With two full coffee cups in her hands, she turned and bumped her hip against his. "Better move out of the way, cowboy, or one of us'll get burned."

When he stepped aside, she set the cups on the table, then sat, indicating that he should join her, but he remained standing. He was still down. "Charlie? What's wrong."

Instead of answering, he walked over to the window and gazed out into the darkness, his hands in his back pockets, his back to her. After a while he said, "I had the afternoon off, so I walked all around the town. Played some slots, went into some stores. I passed a big magazine stand. My word, there were hundreds of them, about all kinds of stuff, cars and machines and flowers and houses. There was one whole row of angry-looking naked ladies." He angled his head around to face her, frowning. "That's not right, that kids can walk by that and see that, is it?"

Cassie shrugged. "A lot of people agree with you. But a lot of others say that freedom of speech comes with some trade-offs."

He shook his head sadly, then returned his gaze to the window. "Doesn't seem right. Back home, Mr. Soames, the barber, he has a locked cabinet where he keeps pictures like that. Not out on the street, and not for kids."

"Is that what's bothering you, Charlie?" she asked softly. "That children are exposed to things they're not ready for?"

"Maybe."

He turned around and ran a finger along the edge of the counter, obviously deep in thought. Again it was a while before he spoke. "Then I went to the library."

Silhouette authors will refresh you

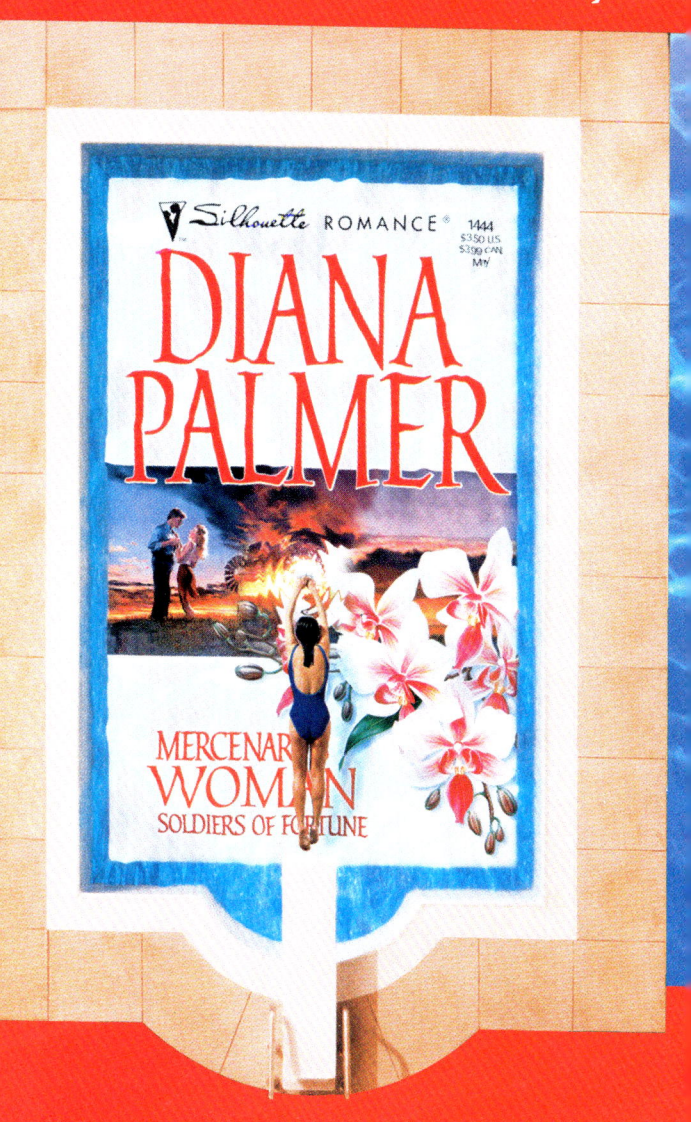

Silhouette ROMANCE® 1444

DIANA PALMER

MERCENARY WOMAN
SOLDIERS OF FORTUNE

We'd like to send you **2 FREE** books and a surprise gift to introduce you to Silhouette Romance®.
Accept our special offer today and
Get Ready for a totally Refreshing Experience!

HOW TO QUALIFY:

1. With a coin, carefully scratch off the silver area on the card at right to see what we have for you—2 FREE BOOKS and a FREE GIFT—ALL YOURS! ALL FREE!

2. Send back the card and you'll receive two brand-new Silhouette Romance® novels. These books have a cover price of $3.99 each in the U.S. and $4.50 each in Canada, but they are yours to keep absolutely free!

3. There's no catch. You're under no obligation to buy anything. We charge nothing—ZERO—for your first shipment and you don't have to make any minimum number of purchases—not even one!

4. The fact is, thousands of readers enjoy receiving books by mail from the Silhouette Reader Service®. They enjoy the convenience of home delivery...they like getting the best new novels at discount prices, BEFORE they're available in stores...and they love their *Heart to Heart* subscriber newsletter featuring author news, horoscopes, recipes, book reviews and much more!

5. We hope that after receiving your free books you'll want to remain a subscriber. But the choice is yours—to continue or cancel, any time at all. So why not take us up on our invitation with no risk of any kind. You'll be glad you did!

SPECIAL FREE GIFT!

We can't tell you what it is...but we're sure you'll like it!
A FREE gift just for giving the Silhouette Reader Service® a try!

Visit us at
www.eHarlequin.com

The **2 FREE BOOKS** we send you will be selected from **SILHOUETTE ROMANCE®**, the series that brings you...a more traditional romance from first love to forever.

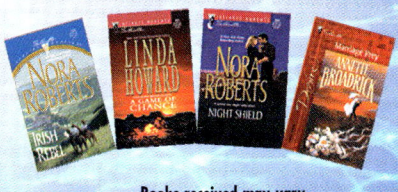

Books received may vary.

▼ DETACH AND MAIL CARD TODAY! ▼

Scratch off the silver area to see what the Silhouette Reader Service has for you.

Silhouette®
Where love comes alive™

YES!
I have scratched off the silver area above. Please send me the **2 FREE** books and gift for which I qualify. I understand I am under no obligation to purchase any books, as explained on the back and on the opposite page.

315 SDL DH46   215 SDL DH45

FIRST NAME

LAST NAME

ADDRESS

APT.#

CITY

STATE/PROV.

ZIP/POSTAL CODE

©2001 HARLEQUIN ENTERPRISES LTD. ® and TM are trademarks owned by Harlequin Enterprises Ltd.

(S-R-04/02)

Offer limited to one per household and not valid to current Silhouette Romance® subscribers. All orders subject to approval.

THE SILHOUETTE READER SERVICE® —Here's how it works:

Accepting your 2 free books and gift places you under no obligation to buy anything. You may keep the books and gift and return the shipping statement marked "cancel." If you do not cancel, about a month later we'll send you 6 additional books and bill you just $3.15 each in the U.S., or $3.50 each in Canada, plus 25¢ shipping & handling per book and applicable taxes if any.* That's the complete price and — compared to cover prices of $3.99 each in the U.S. and $4.50 each in Canada — it's quite a bargain! You may cancel at any time, but if you choose to continue, every month we'll send you 6 more books, which you may either purchase at the discount price or return to us and cancel your subscription.

*Terms and prices subject to change without notice. Sales tax applicable in N.Y. Canadian residents will be charged applicable provincial taxes and GST.

DETACH AND MAIL CARD TODAY!

If offer card is missing write to: Silhouette Reader Service, 3010 Walden Ave., P.O. Box 1867, Buffalo NY 14240-1867

BUSINESS REPLY MAIL
FIRST-CLASS MAIL   PERMIT NO. 717-003   BUFFALO, NY

POSTAGE WILL BE PAID BY ADDRESSEE

SILHOUETTE READER SERVICE
3010 WALDEN AVE
PO BOX 1867
BUFFALO NY 14240-9952

NO POSTAGE
NECESSARY
IF MAILED
IN THE
UNITED STATES

"It's not a very big one, is it?"

"It isn't? It sure seemed like a powerful lot of books to me. I thought maybe there'd be a book or something on how to rescue—I mean, help you."

Cassie chuckled, then took a sip of her coffee. "Did you find that book?"

His answering smile was brief and rueful. "No. But I stayed a while, anyway. I thought I might study some."

"What did you want to study?"

He shrugged. "It's silly."

"Tell me."

He leaned against the kitchen counter and stared somewhere off in space. "I wanted to get a handle on what it's like today that's different from back home, different from the time I live in. I have all these questions, like what happened to horses when cars got popular, and how did you ladies go from wearing long skirts to short ones. And when did the prairies disappear and all these buildings get put in their place."

"Wow. That's a lot to take in, in one visit."

He nodded in agreement. "I hardly knew where to begin."

He really was in quite a pensive, melancholy mood. Somehow Cassie sensed not to push it, that if he wanted to tell her what was really bothering him, he'd come out with it.

"Have you thought about getting your Cowboy Charlie stories published?" he asked abruptly.

The change of subject startled her, and she set her coffee cup down. "How did we get on that?"

He met her gaze directly now, no longer in his dream-like state. "I looked through the children's section at the library. Your stories and your pictures are as good as any there."

"I think you may be prejudiced."

"I am not. You're good, Cassie, really good."

She felt uncomfortable with his compliments. Sure, she liked her stories, but didn't think they were professional caliber. And she knew she had some artistic talent, but she was untrained. Her drawings left her in despair much of the time—there were pictures in her head that she couldn't get down on paper, or couldn't get down as well as she'd like to.

"Don't, Charlie," she said. "Maybe one day, but not yet."

"Have I upset you?"

"It's just that if I could, I'd study art and take some writing classes and get better. Then maybe I'd dare to try to get someone to publish my stories. Maybe."

"Why don't you take those classes?"

"Money. Time. Trish. My salary doesn't cover our expenses, so I do some hand calligraphy invitations at night, and lately there haven't been any to do. My car needs work, I'm barely keeping the roof over our heads as it is, and I don't have the luxury to indulge in self-improvement dreams." It had come out a lot stronger than she intended; now she sat back in her chair and sighed. "Sorry. Didn't mean to get so carried away."

"No, I'm the one who's sorry," Charlie said, and came toward her.

She held up a hand to stop any further apologies. "Please, let's not go there, not tonight." She waved away her own sadness and decided to do some subject changing herself. "Hey, you going to sit or not? Your coffee will get cold. Or maybe you want something stronger? I have some brandy somewhere."

"Better not." He gazed at her for another long moment, took in a deep breath, then surprised her by getting onto his knees next to her chair. One of her hands was on her lap and he covered it with one of his. "I didn't mean to upset you."

How strong his hand was, how small her own felt in comparison. "Not your fault. It was just a button you pushed, that's all."

He continued to stare at her, looking deeply into her eyes, as though memorizing them. "You want to know what's on my mind?" he asked softly. "What's making me sorrowful?"

"Yes. Please."

"You. Eating hot dogs with you and Trish. Taking her on the Ferris wheel ride. Being invited for dinner this week. Being here with you, tonight, talking about all these thoughts I have, knowing you'll listen and won't laugh at me. Looking at your face, your mouth, your beautiful eyes, I get to dreaming about...things that can't be."

A shudder ran through her as Cassie's eyes filled with sudden moisture. "Oh, Charlie. I know."

"The thing is...I didn't know it would feel this way."

"What would?"

"Love."

The word hung in the air for a moment before he went on.

"Love," he repeated. "It hurts. It hurts real bad."

A couple of tears escaped and trickled down her cheek, and she used her free hand to swipe them away. "Charlie, don't. Please."

"I know, but I had to—"

The ringing phone startled Cassie so much that she gasped. "Damn," she muttered. There were entirely too many bells in her life! she thought, as she jumped up and reached for the receiver hanging on the wall next to the sink. "Yes?" she barked.

"Mommy?"

It was her daughter, and she was crying. Cassie's own tears dried up in an instant as her blood froze with immediate and instinctive maternal fear. "What is it, Trish? Tell me. Are you all right?"

"They told me I was a liar."

"Who did?"

"Karen A. and Karen P. and Julie Ann and Marybeth. They said I was lying about Cowboy Charlie."

Cassie's muscles unclenched; she was able to breathe again. She'd just experienced every mother's nightmare—the child calls up in tears of pain, and the mother's mind takes off on all kinds of tangents, from disaster to dismemberment to death.

Not necessary to go there this time, thank you, God, she thought. "What did you tell them about Cowboy Charlie?"

"Well—" she sniffled "—they all know about your stories." She sniffled again. "I mean, I tell them about him all the time, and everyone thinks it's cool that you made him up and that you draw him and all. But I told them he's real now and they called me a liar!"

"What is it?" Charlie stood by her side, concern all over his face.

"Just a minute, honey. Shall I put Charlie on the phone?"

"He's there?"

She handed the phone to Charlie.

"Hi, Trish, what's up?" He listened, saying "Uh-huh" once and "Yup" another time, then nodded. "Your momma and I will be right over."

He hung up the phone. "We have to go to Lisa's house. We can't have anyone call Trish a liar."

"But—"

"Coming?" As though a finger had been snapped, the depressed Charlie was a thing of the past. The man of action was back. "If you're not, tell me where it is. I got my vest and chaps in your garage. My spurs and six-shooters, too. I'll get them while you dress. You with me? Good. Let's go."

Lisa's house, Charlie noted, was a lot bigger than Cassie's, and downright elegant, if you went for that kind of thing. Cassie had told him that the man of the house was a lawyer and his wife ran a catering business, and they had a lot of money but weren't stuck-up at all. There was a spacious, green lawn and lots of blooming flowers all the way up the path to the door. When Charlie rang the doorbell, a young couple answered and introduced themselves as Richard and Ann Thomas, then ushered him and Cassie inside.

"Hi, ladies," Charlie said by way of welcome to the circle of girl children who sat all around the large room to the right of the doorway. A lot more than children were in that room; apart from the couches, tables and lamps, there were sleeping bags, blankets, pillows and dolls scattered about. Pretty-colored wrapping paper dotted the place. The smell of wieners and mustard and roasted marshmallows was in the air.

A group of seven-year-olds gazed up at him, most of them with wide-eyed wonder. But there was one little skeptic, a pinch-faced child with a horse tail on each side of her head and missing front teeth. "Are you really Cowboy Charlie?"

"That's what they call me."

"I don't believe you."

"That's your right."

Another piped up. "Are those guns real?"

Charlie walked farther into the room. "They sure are. There are no bullets in them, of course. You should never walk around with bullets in your gun, right?"

"Right," came a chorus of rapt little girls.

Charlie put both hands on the gun handles, whipped them out, twirled them one way and then the other, then slid them back into their holsters, all in a matter of seconds.

"Wow." This was spoken by a little girl with her thumb in her mouth, but who was clearly audible, despite that.

"Anyone got a rope?" Charlie asked, and was supplied with a piece of clothesline. Charlie did some twirling tricks, some more gun spinning. He let the little girls try on his hat and walk around in his boots.

Then he sat down in the middle of the circle, with Trish sitting triumphantly on his lap, and told them about the time his horse, Felicity, hurt his leg and how the doc wanted to put him down, but Charlie wrapped it in some special eucalyptus leaves an Indian had told him about and then turned him out to pasture for a while so he could heal himself.

The children were enthralled. Even the little cynic became a believer. They were just about the cutest bunch of little ones, Charlie decided, in their ruffled pajamas and nightgowns with funny drawings and designs on them. And they wanted more stories, so he told them about the time Miz Cunningham, who ran the candy shop, accused little Pablo Garcia of stealing, and it turned out to be Miz Cunningham's boy Ronald who did it. That made Charlie mad, so he insisted both mother and son apologize and give Pablo a licorice whip every day for a month.

Cassie was as enthralled as the children, especially during the second story. She hadn't written that one, so she assumed he had lived it. She'd have to ask him if he'd like to collaborate with her on bringing it to the pages of her rapidly growing pile of stories.

Richard Thomas, Lisa's dad, a barrel-chested man with a careful haircut, stood on Cassie's left in the living room archway entrance, his arms folded across his chest, his head nodding his appreciation. After a while he turned to Cassie and said, "He's good. He a pro? Are birthday parties his specialty? I'd be glad to recommend him to some people."

"No," she answered. "Charlie's just who he says he is. A cowboy."

Ann Thomas, on her right, wore a huge grin on her pretty face. "Well he's a godsend. I thought we were going to erupt into a small war before he came."

"I'm sorry Trish was so insistent," Cassie said. "I hope it didn't spoil Lisa's birthday party."

"Are you kidding? She'll be the toast of the school after this. He's kind of a hunk, huh?" she added, *sotto voce,* so her husband wouldn't hear.

"Kinda."

"I take it he's in town for the rodeo."

Cassie smiled, but didn't answer—it was all too complicated to explain and besides, why bother? The truth was too farfetched. Earlier in the week she'd met a close friend for coffee and had started to tell her all about Charlie. She'd stopped when her friend began to stare at her as though trying to decide whether or not to commit her. The parents would be as disbelieving as her friend—and the little girls—had been. And who could blame any one of them?

It was at least a half hour later when Charlie stood up and stretched. He let out a huge yawn, scratched his head and said, "All right, young ladies. It's way past my bedtime, so I guess it must be way past yours, too. Time to hit the sack." He glanced over at a wall clock. "My, it's nearly eleven."

A couple of the children joined Charlie in his yawn. "But, Charlie—" protested another.

"No, we have to get some sleep. All of us."

Ann Thomas clapped her hands, walking into the room as she did. "Let's everybody thank Cowboy Charlie."

A chorus of thank-yous and hugs followed. Another of the children asked, "Are you going to be in the rodeo tomorrow?"

"Nope."

"How about the last day, Monday?"

"Well, I hadn't planned..."

Charlie let the sentence peter out as a brilliant notion sprang into his head. The rodeo. Of course. There was prize money to be won. Maybe that's why he was here! He was supposed to enter the rodeo, win and give the money to Cassie. That way she wouldn't need to have her mortgage extended, she could pay some months in advance! She could even take classes and study and be what she wanted to be, a professional writer!

"Yep," he said. "I'll be there tomorrow and on the Fourth of July too."

"What?" Cassie said, startled.

Charlie looked around at the eager faces. "Why don't you all come, if your folks'll let you, and cheer me on?"

An excited burst came from the partygoers. Charlie waved his hat at them all. "Gotta go, young ladies."

"Wait, Charlie!" This was Trish, tugging on his elbow.

He looked down at her.

"One more good-night kiss?" she asked, and he knew she was doing it to take possession of him, to show the others—the doubters—that she had indeed produced Cowboy Charlie and he was hers.

That she was, more than she could know.

He leaned over and pointed to his cheek. "Put one right there, partner."

As soon as she did, all the other children had to put one there, too, and Trish was gracious enough to allow it. However, she clung to him one last time and whispered in his ear, "I'll be home tomorrow night. Will you read me a story then?"

"I most certainly will," Charlie whispered back. "Count on it."

Finally it was time to leave. Charlie grabbed Cassie's hand and headed for the door. A plate with a huge wedge of birthday cake was pressed into Cassie's free hand, and then Charlie and Cassie were outside in the cool night air.

The smell of freshly mown grass assaulted her nostrils. Somewhere nearby someone was barbecuing, and that smell mingled in with the other. Two of her favorite summer aromas in the world, but she barely noticed.

"Are you crazy?" she said to Charlie as they walked down the path to her car. "How can you enter the rodeo? I don't know anything about it, but aren't they professional? How can you win over professionals?"

"I know it sounds crazy, but I'm pretty sure it's the answer." He went on enthusiastically while she unlocked the car and set the cake on the back seat. "It's what I'm supposed to do. Maybe I'll win a prize or two, who knows? But that's why I'm here. That's the answer."

With a whoop of joy, Charlie put his hands around Cassie's waist, jerked her off the ground and twirled her around, several times, until she was dizzy from spinning and from laughing.

"Charlie, put me down!"

"Soon, my darlin', soon." Then he spun her some more, so she closed her eyes and just gave in to it. It felt wonderful, to be held in strong arms and spun around in the moonlight.

When he finally did lower her, he held her to him till she caught her breath. Oh, how good he felt, with his arms around her, pulling her tight. He kissed her ear, then rested his cheek on the top of her head.

"So, darlin', what do you think of my scheme?"

His scheme.

That was it, that word was what was wrong with this picture.

Teddy had embarked on all kinds of foolish schemes, leading to one failure after another. What Charlie was proposing sounded suspiciously like one of Teddy's "projects"—to triumph over incredible odds and win the day.

She shook her head. Another one, she thought. One more dreamer. Was it her fate to attract men who dreamed and didn't deliver?

"What do you think?" Charlie asked her again, his voice still brimming with enthusiasm.

Cassie didn't have the heart to say what she really felt. Men and their flaky schemes! Or some men and their flaky schemes, anyway. But she wasn't going to throw water on his happiness, not tonight. That wouldn't be fair.

"I think that we'd better get going, is what I think. The coffee's still hot and I want some of that birthday cake!"

Chapter Seven

After saying good-night to Cassie, Charlie had trouble sleeping. He was excited, revved up, as the modern expression went, wanting to get going with his plans. Before dawn early Sunday morning, Charlie began walking toward the fairgrounds, figuring he'd be able to get the lay of the land as to how a person entered all these contests he intended to enter, and win, of course.

More and more this felt like the obvious thing to do. He had no higher education or special training, didn't know how to operate any modern machinery—although he probably could learn if he was taught—but, by heaven, he knew animals! Knew their moods and how to get around them, knew what to do to make them give out with the best they could. He could ride and rope and sit the most stubborn horse or the craziest bull.

Those were his skills, maybe not much by the day's

standards, but just what the doctor ordered for a rodeo competition.

The desert was beautiful at night, chilled and mysterious, with sounds of murmuring and rustling that always set his senses tingling. A breeze abraded his cheeks, and as he walked along, he felt filled with both peace and energy. More than that—purpose. He was a man who needed to know where he was headed, so he could do the best job he could.

As the star-filled, black sky began to lighten over the eastern mountain range, Charlie noted the fine layer of mist that covered the prairie like a blanket of gray wool. He inhaled deeply. God, he loved this country, these open spaces! Much preferred them to town life, which was too busy, too fast, too filled with people and noise and clutter. Cassie had told him if he thought Yatesboro was busy, he wouldn't have been able to tolerate the nearby city of Reno. And New York? Why, she figured he'd run screaming for the hills, never to be heard from again.

Cassie. Just the woman's name brought a smile to his lips. She was a singular, special woman, for sure. Fiery and fierce, protective and sarcastic. Funny, too. Complicated, that's what Cassie was, but his heart sure got a little lifting feeling when he thought about her.

It was love, for certain. He'd never felt this way before and it seemed to take up much of the available space in his chest area.

But there was still room for that aching feeling, too, when he thought about how he would have to leave her...if he was successful, that is. And he aimed to be successful, despite that ache in his heart, because that's why he'd been sent here.

Squaring his shoulders, Charlie picked up his pace. It was, he figured, twenty miles or so to the fairgrounds from Cassie's place, so he still had a far piece to go.

Just as the topmost crest of the sun was making an appearance, a dusty pickup truck slowed down next to him, and a voice said, "Going to the rodeo grounds?"

Charlie turned to see a large, red-faced man in a Stetson grinning at him from behind the wheel. "Sure am."

"Hop in, I'll give you a lift."

"Appreciate it."

His name was Kyle Bartlett, he told Charlie, and he was one of the ranchers supplying animals for the rodeo contests. He was proud of his stock and of his spread, two thousand or so acres that had been in his family for six generations.

Kyle was talkative, which was good, because Charlie had a lot of questions to ask. But he knew to approach it slowly. It was the way of the West.

"Sure is a beautiful day," Charlie told him when Kyle had slowed down to take himself a breath.

"That it is. You from around here?" Kyle asked him.

"Visiting," he told him.

"Where from?"

"Up north." He figured that was as good an answer as any. "I was here on Friday night," he went on, changing the subject. "Mighty fine carnival. And I saw some fancy horseflesh, too. You all put on a real good show."

"Yep, we work hard once a year. 'Course we can't complete with the big-time rodeos, like the National

Finals down in Vegas or the one up in Calgary. Ever been to that one?"

"No, sir."

"Now *that's* a show they put on in Calgary. They're professionals. But I like to think we have some pretty good folks competing here in our little town."

"From what I saw, I agree. That Roland Hawkins, he was mighty impressive."

Kyle chuckled. "Yes, Rollie's good, when he's sober enough to stay on a horse, that is." He shook his large head. "Poor Rollie. Last year he got disqualified because he decided the bull's butt was its head, and no one could tell him any different."

Charlie joined Kyle in a good laugh, then figured he could get more to the point. "I'm aiming to do a little bull riding myself, while I'm here. And I promise you I know which end of that bull is up."

"Really? You a rodeo man?"

"Just for fun, after-roundup type of thing. But I'd like to give yours a try. That's why I'm going there today. To find out what I got to do to enter."

"Probably not much of anything, today, at least, friend. Sorry. Maybe you can enter an event for tomorrow, although only if there's a slot or two available."

"Oh?"

"Can't just show up and sign up the same day. We got to see your ID, look you up on the computer, see if you're okay."

"The computer?"

"Yeah. We got all these rules we have to follow." His grin was apologetic. "The lawyers make us do it because we've been sued a couple times, so we have to watch our backs. No felons are allowed to compete. And no professionals—here in Yatesboro we've agreed to keep it amateur. You know, only folks who don't ride the rodeo circuit for a living."

"Well, I'm sure an amateur, anyway." Charlie frowned. This was going to be more difficult than he'd thought.

He was deep into his musings when they pulled into the huge parking lot on the grounds. "Much obliged, Kyle," Charlie said, shaking the older man's hand after he'd opened his door to alight. "I'll just see what can be done."

"Welcome, whatever happens. And good luck."

What hit him right away was the smell. Gasoline, for sure. But also dust and manure and coffee and hay. It was a fine smell, a roundup smell, and Charlie closed his eyes and inhaled deeply. He was home; at least more at home than he had been the entire week.

Over on a long table there was a big pot of coffee and some paper cups next to it, so he went and poured himself a cup. His stomach growled, but there didn't seem to be any grub around, so he figured he'd get himself a huge steak breakfast later on in town.

No one asked him who he was or if he belonged there, which was a good sign. Sipping his coffee, he wandered around some, noting that everyone on the grounds was dressed like he was, which gave him a sense of kinship that he'd been missing for days.

Home. He missed it something fierce. Missed the smells, the quiet, the simplicity. Was it simple back home, he had to wonder, because Cassie had made it that way for him? Or were those truly simpler times?

Simpler...and not so lonely. Yes, except for Cassie and Trish, he'd never felt so lonely in his life as he had since he'd come to life in this modern time. He felt lonely working at the store, walking the streets, in the midst of the crowds. Back home, even if there was no one around for miles, he was never lonely.

Charlie refilled his coffee cup and walked over to the stable area where there was a small outbuilding and a hand-painted sign saying Registration. Sipping his coffee some more, and grateful for its potency, Charlie geared himself up. Kyle had told him he'd need a driver's license or some form of ID to register. ID, he gathered, was short for identification, and he had not a thing on him that could identify him as anyone. Heck, he didn't even know his last name, which was a pretty sorry state of affairs.

He'd have to do some fancy talking if he was to get anywhere near the inside of that arena.

By midafternoon when Cassie finally spotted Charlie up ahead, trudging toward town, she sped up. He had a saddle slung over his left shoulder, and it looked heavy to her, although his pace was regular and he didn't seem to be staggering under the weight. As if, she thought. Her Charlie never staggered. But his head was down, as though he was deep in thought. Or dejected.

Had his crazy scheme, which sounded like something out of an old Judy Garland/Mickey Rooney movie, fallen through?

She drove past him, checked traffic in both directions, executed a perfect *U,* and pulled up behind him. Rolling down the passenger window, she honked once, then yelled, "Hey, cowboy."

He wheeled around. "Cassie!"

At the sight of her, his face lit up like the proverbial

Christmas tree, and she couldn't help noticing a corresponding surge of joy in response. It felt great to have a man glad to see you, and felt even better to experience the rush of pleasure she felt in his presence. She'd had no idea how starved she'd been for this.

"What a coincidence. What're you doing here?" Charlie asked her, heading back toward her.

"Giving you a lift, silly, and it's not a coincidence. When I woke up this morning, I realized you didn't have any way to get here and probably had to walk the whole way."

He was at the driver's side of the car now, and leaned one elbow on the open window frame. With his tanned face this close to her, the pitty-pat in her heart sped up even more.

"I'm sure grateful." His eyes twinkled, the turquoise color paler, yet more vivid, in the afternoon sunlight.

"Why didn't you let me drive you this morning?"

He lifted a shoulder. "You needed a good lying-in. You work hard all week. Besides, I got a ride partway from a rancher."

"Oh. Well then, good. Hop in."

Instead he grinned at her. "You sure do look pretty today." He pushed a curl off her cheek and wound it around her ear. At his touch her skin did a little dance of excitement.

"Yep," he continued. "Pretty and fresh and soft. I like you without all the paint. Mind you, you're pretty with the paint, too."

She lowered her gaze. "You're just saying nice things to me because you're glad not to have to walk."

"Nope. I'm saying those nice things to you because I mean them." He grinned again. "But, I'm also glad to see you. This here saddle is heavy." He opened the back door and set his saddle down on the seat. "Where's Trish?"

"Still at Lisa's. I'm picking her up later. That poor mother is taking the kids to a movie—can you imagine? After a night like that, ten giggling little girls, ten popcorns and drinks, ten little trips to the bathroom. Heaven help her. And by tonight, Trish will be so tired, she'll be a monster."

"Not Trish. Never." He sat down next to her, closed the passenger door, and they took off. He worked on his seat belt, muttering, "Damn thing is harder'n..." but he finally got it buckled.

"So how was it?" she asked him. "Where'd you get the saddle?"

"Fella lent it to me, the one who gave me a lift. I'm not even sure if I'll be using it, but I figured I'd best be prepared."

"So you're registered to compete, then?"

"I hope so." He shook his head. "I tell you, Cassie, entering a rodeo sure was different in my day, not nearly so complicated. I had to put the tips of my fingers on this ink thing and then on paper because I didn't have a driver's license."

"Fingerprints. That's for identification purposes."

"So they told me."

She chuckled. "Won't they be surprised when you don't turn up on any database known to modern man."

Charlie seemed not to have heard her. "My word, what if someone doesn't drive or can't afford a car—what does he do to prove he exists? And the entrance fee took up most of the money I've earned this week. Not that more would have done me any good." He shot her a rueful look. "I don't have my own horse, so that kind of narrows the possibilities."

"Oh, Charlie, what a shame. Can't we borrow a horse for you, or rent one?"

He shook his head. "It's not as simple as just riding. There's a connection between a good cow pony and the rider, and it can't happen overnight. It takes years."

Cassie glanced over at her passenger, to see if he had that same expression that Teddy used to get, the discontented one that said his dreams were not going to come true, the fantasy that had been fueling him, making him glow from within, was history. Her husband's face used to look like someone had turned the lights out.

But Charlie didn't seem overly upset. More thoughtful, really. "I sure wish Felicity had made it here with me. He is about the best-trained animal. He can sense what I need almost before I do, his moves are quicker than a lightning bug. And he's loyal and good-natured, too." He smiled at her. "You came up with a good one, there, Cassie. A man couldn't ask for a better horse."

"You really miss her, don't you? I mean him."

"Yep." Now he did frown. "I worry about him too. What's happening to him if I'm not there? Is someone feeding him, exercising him? By any chance, do you know?"

"I have no idea. There's so much I don't know about how this works, Charlie. I'm so sorry."

Sensing her distress, he patted her arm. "Well, never you mind. I'm sure he's being looked after.

This is not the first time something like this has happened, after all.''

Cassie couldn't help observing that she wasn't even questioning this conversation about a horse in another dimension. So totally had she accepted Charlie's other life and his present existence in hers, they could have been discussing a beloved relative in another town instead of a fictional horse. That was how day-to-day they sounded.

When they got to the edge of town, Charlie requested that she stop at the hardware store so he could make a couple of purchases. When he got back to the car, he said, ''All right if I use your yard to work on this saddle? It needs oiling and a little repair.''

''Sure.''

Good. She wasn't ready to say goodbye to him yet. And, as Trish was taken care of, she didn't have to.

At her place she said, ''Hungry?''

''Starving.''

''Get washed up, I'll bring some lunch out to the picnic table.'' A few minutes later she came out to the backyard with several large sandwiches, a couple of bottles of pop and her sketchbook.

''Food's here when you want it,'' she told him, settling herself on one of the benches that went with the redwood table. ''Mind if I doodle while you work?''

''Fine.''

He had the saddle up on an old, paint-spattered work table next to the garage. And, she couldn't help noticing, he'd taken his shirt off. Oh, my, she thought, with a silent sigh. My and my again. He was a sight, all glistening, sun-bronzed skin over a well-developed chest, long, sculpted arms covered lightly with blond hair. The muscles of his biceps and forearms contracted and expanded with each move of the cloth over the saddle, and his back muscles rippled. There was not the slightest suggestion of love handles on the man. Charlie was a hunk.

She'd never drawn him nude, but if she had he would have looked just like this. The incarnation of a female's fantasy. Cassie suppressed a sigh and had to swallow down the most incredible urge to undo his jeans, just to see if the rest of him matched her imagination.

"Come," she said. "Eat."

He wiped his hands on a cloth, then joined her at the table but didn't sit down. Several huge bites in a row told her he really was hungry, but she enjoyed watching the play of muscles in his jaw as he chewed, noted the trickle of sweat wending its way between his pectorals, along the thin line of hair beneath, and disappearing into his trousers. She gulped, and was afraid it was audible.

To get her mind off that, she took a bite of her sandwich, then picked up her sketchbook. Charlie polished off his drink and went back to work.

"So, tell me about what it's like back home, where you live. What your rodeos are like." Her pencil began to outline a new picture of Charlie, based on the model she had in front of her. "How did rodeos start? I have a purpose here, you know."

"Do you?"

"Background for 'Charlie and the Rodeo.' What do you think?"

"Don't mind in the least." He looked up from his saddle work and grinned. "Do I win?"

"That remains to be seen. Talk to me, okay?"

Cassie focused on the careful, deliberate movement of his hands on the tough old leather, and she tried to copy them as she listened.

"Well, heck," he said laconically, "I'm pretty sure it started as just a little fun between cowboys. See, on a roundup, you work your tail off. By the end of the day, you're so worn-out, all you got left is the energy to brag. You know how men are, we get to comparing ourselves with one another."

"So I've noticed," she said dryly.

"The men would get to arguing about who's the best rider or the fastest roper, or who had that knack of staying on some crazy horse who'd buck you from here to the moon, if you let him. And all this bragging and comparing would go on for nights, so that at the end of the roundup, they'd lay down bets, and everybody would gather around and there'd be a roping and a riding contest to settle the issue."

"So that's where it started. Men bragging and betting."

"I suppose. But then it got bigger. Maybe a bunch of hands working for one ranch would hear about some ornery, impossible-to-ride horse at another ranch down the road. They'd head on over there on a Sunday and round up that horse, and maybe three or four more just as ornery. And there'd be some more bragging and some more betting, and sure enough, there'd be a contest between the two ranches. Of course, the buster is the one who wins, because he has the most experience."

"The buster?"

"He's the fella who goes from ranch to ranch breaking wild horses for ranch work. Naturally, he can break a bronco better than a local man. Anyhow, that's how it started, I guess."

This was great stuff, Cassie thought. She really hadn't done much research on the world in which she'd set her Cowboy Charlie stories, because she hadn't intended him to be an authentic cowboy from the Old West. From what she'd read, that breed had been composed of smelly, illiterate, crude, rude and often violent men who were much more comfortable with animals and isolation than with society. Her Charlie was a glamorized, sanitized, attractive version, more suitable to children's stories, in her opinion, anyway.

But maybe it was time to do more research, give her stories a little more veracity, more reality, more depth. In fact, if she took herself and her stories more seriously....

Her musings were interrupted by a muttered oath from Charlie, one she'd never heard from him. "Will you look at this?" He pointed to the saddle horn. "See, this isn't what I think of as a saddle, not a real one. But they got all these rules. It has to have a fourteen-inch swell and five-inch cantle, but there's nothing about it to anchor a rider." He shook his head, muttering, "Rules, rules, rules. No wonder people nowadays go plum crazy. Look at these."

He pulled a sheaf of papers out of his back pocket and gave them to Cassie. He picked up another sandwich and bit into it while she scanned the papers, reading parts of it aloud. "'...must leave the chute with both feet in the stirrups and both spurs against the horse's shoulders...must scratch ahead for the first five jumps, then behind.'" She scanned the page. "Wow, lots of fine print. A rider gets disqualified if he's 'bucked off, changes hands on the rein, wraps the rein around the hand, pulls leather or blows a stirrup, touches the animal or saddle or rein with his free hand or rides with locked spurs or touches the horse with his hat.'"

She looked over at Charlie, who took another bite of his sandwich, followed by a swallow of pop.

"I see what you mean," she told him. "It's complicated."

"Not only that. There's all these other 'thou shalt nots.' You can move this way, can't move that, four seconds here but only two seconds there. It's enough to make a man run for the hills."

"We do have a lot of rules, don't we," she agreed. "It's called civilization, I guess."

"Rules," he snorted derisively, shaking his head as he went back to polishing the leather till it shone. "Back home, we don't have these kind of rules. And when you go to a rodeo? There's no chutes and no fences."

"No chutes? Really?"

"No, ma'am. You get those animals into a pen and you get yourself one judge and that's all you need. It's a simple system, and it works. Nowadays, you got to have timers and ticket sellers and contractors who bring in the animals. Judges, pickup men, flag men."

She'd never seen him quite so irritated; one more glimpse of the many facets of Cowboy Charlie. "It's a business, Charlie. And it's the American way—if something is fun and attracts a crowd, find out how to make money on it."

He straightened, pushed his hat back and scratched his head, causing several strands of blond hair to fall over one eye. He seemed to be looking somewhere in the distance when he said, "I was thinking, early this morning, about how it used to be so simple."

"Nothing is simple, Charlie. If it ever was."

"So it seems."

"Progress. The good news and the bad." She needed, suddenly, to explain it to him, to defend her existence and the world she lived in. "You get penicillin to fight disease and then new diseases come along that resist penicillin. You get drought-resistant corn and then the trees start dying. You get computers to make communication more easy and people stop writing real letters. It's all a trade-off, Charlie. It's the way things are done."

His gaze was troubled as he looked at her. "How do you stand it?"

She shrugged. "It's what I'm used to, I guess."

She rose from the bench and walked over to him. Pushing the errant strands of hair off his sweaty face, she said, "You must be in a deep culture shock, Charlie. I wish I could help. It's too much for anyone to take in."

He stared down at her, then set his rag down. Lightly, as though afraid to get her face dirty, he cupped her cheeks. "You make it okay," he said softly.

Her breathing stopped. Lord, he was close; she was eye level with his gleaming chest and its firm ridge of muscle, and he smelled of warm sunshine and sweat. She craned her neck to gaze up at him. Her voice rich with emotion, she murmured, "I don't know what to do when you say mushy things like that."

"Nothing to do. Nothing to say, either." One side

of his mouth lifted in a small smile. "I love you," he said softly.

He waited, as though expecting her to say the words back to him. But she couldn't. There was something so committed, so final about the phrase. Instead she closed her eyes and offered her mouth to him.

For a moment their lips were joined in a sweet, tender kiss. But only for a moment, before the kiss became stronger, more hungry, more demanding. Charlie broke it off, backing away from her. "This is too damned hard," he growled.

Shaking with desire, Cassie almost asked him to take her, right there on the picnic table, like a scene out of a movie. But even though her body craved it, her mind hadn't followed suit; it felt as if, by not being able to tell him she loved him, she would be offering sex as consolation.

Charlie paced like a restless cat, back and forth by the table where the saddle rested. "Too damned hard," he said again.

She watched him for a few moments, then offered, "I can't imagine how you must feel, Charlie, I mean with all your disappointments. The world and all its complications. And you hoped you'd be able to compete, and now you probably won't be able to—"

"Who says so?"

"I thought—"

"I'm going to be there tomorrow, of course I am." He continued to pace. "I paid my money, didn't I? Signed all their papers and swore up and down it was the truth, didn't I? Which it all was," he added, then frowned. "Far as I know, anyway, these being unusual circumstances."

"To say the least."

His pacing stopped and he looked at her. She grinned at him and, almost grudgingly he grinned back. "To say the least," he echoed, and, like that, the sense of a caged lion was gone from his attitude. Ruefully he picked up his cloth again and went back to work on the saddle.

Cassie perched on the table this time, her feet on a bench, and forgot about drawing. All she wanted to do was watch him.

"Oh," he said, after a bit, "I gave your name and address as a contact. Okay?"

"Sure."

"Plus, I gave myself a last name. A middle one too. I hope you don't mind."

"You what?" Her mouth dropped open with surprise.

"Charles Lloyd Culpepper. What do you think?"

She took a minute to mull it over, then nodded. "It sounds authentic, anyway. How did that happen?"

"I had to come up with something pretty quick, or all those dang papers weren't going to go through. The trucks, out there at the fairgrounds? One of them said Lloyd's Hay and Feed, and another said Culpepper Plumbing Services and Portable Toilets."

Her laugh erupted from deep inside, and Charlie's answering grin said he was pleased to have made her laugh this time. "Now all I can do," he said, "is hope that if this is what I'm supposed to do, it'll all come out all right. If it's not, something else will come along, I guess. See, I figure we got to get you relaxed about that mortgage so you can spend more time on your stories and your drawing."

"Charlie, truly, it's not your responsibility."

The determination was back in his eye. "Well, sure it is. That's why I'm here, remember?"

"How can I forget?"

Something made her glance at her watch, and she started. "Oops. Talk about forgetting. I have to pick up Trish," she said, jumping down from the tabletop, gathering her sketch pad and the plates. "And then we're off to a barbecue. Would you like to come along? They're nice people, and they always serve huge sides of beef and terrific coleslaw."

Charlie watched her flurry of activity, sorry the warm, close afternoon with Cassie was over. Now there was a child to pick up, a party invitation.

And he wanted to go, oh, yes. The thought of a barbecue and all that grub, the prospect of another precious evening with Cassie and Trish was sorely tempting.

But Cassie's reaction to his dreams for her—that she take her writing and art seriously—and her obvious lack of confidence in herself, had set another idea hopping in his head. This, too, was why he'd been sent here, for sure.

So, no, he couldn't go to the barbecue. He had other plans for that time period. It involved being alone in Cassie's house without her looking on, and then making use of Miz Lorna's back door key and the copy machine she had in her office, the one she had taught him to use just the other day.

Chapter Eight

When Cassie and Trish came home that night, there was a note from Charlie on the table by the front door. In block letters he had printed, "Come out to the rodeo tomorrow and cheer me on." It was signed CLP.

The writing was crude, and Cassie realized she had never seen a sample of Charlie's writing; in fact, she couldn't remember if in any of her stories she'd mentioned that he'd been to school or was even literate. He was, it was obvious, able to read and write, which pleased her, but he was just as obviously not formerly schooled beyond a few grades, which also made sense, given the time and area he lived in.

There was still so much she wanted to know about him—his childhood, parents, his interests. The next time they were alone, she would be sure to ask him.

CLP. Charles Lloyd Culpepper. Cassie smiled at Charlie's new monogram. But Trish, who had been looking forward to seeing her hero, was disappointed at Charlie's absence.

"He said he'd read me a story tonight. He promised."

"I know, sweetie. But he has to get his rest for the big day tomorrow. I guess you're just going to have to make do with me, okay?"

As though realizing she'd been whining, Trish smiled apologetically and said, "Sure, Mom."

When her daughter had bathed herself and was in her pajamas, Cassie took one look at her sleepy face and wondered if she'd even stay awake to hear word one of the story. Still, she began her story. "This is about the time that Cowboy Charlie became a real person."

Trish yawned. "But Cowboy Charlie *is* real, Mommy."

"Yes, I know he is, but this is the story that's in my head tonight."

"Okay," her little girl said, and closed her eyes. Within seconds her breathing had become even and deep, and Cassie saw that her audience of one was now asleep. Still she went on with her story for a little while longer, because indeed, she couldn't stop the images forming in her brain.

"Cowboy Charlie became real, for a little while. And he made the woman and her child very happy because he was funny and strong and he told great stories. But he couldn't stay real, because those were the rules. He didn't know who had made up the rules or why they had to be obeyed, only that it was so and there was nothing to be done about it. It made Cowboy Charlie sad and it made the new friends he made sad, too…"

* * *

The cowboys hanging around the corral weren't being too friendly to him, Charlie couldn't help noticing. Not that he blamed them. In the Code of the Old West you couldn't trust anyone you didn't know personally; there were too many escaped convicts, cattle rustlers and general low-lifes who made their way out west, lured by the freedom from civilization, the scarcity of lawmen and the huge expanses of unoccupied land between jurisdictions.

The local men who were contestants today were probably descended from the original settlers, so Charlie represented the unknown, the intruder, and he understood that. Still, he was unfailingly polite to all, and managed to get to talking with Sam Milton, one of the professional rodeo clowns the town hired for its yearly event. From what Sam told him, you didn't want any amateurs doing his job, which was to protect the riders, most especially from the wrath of a raging bull.

The bull had only two things in mind—to get free of the rider on his back and to hook, trample or kill any other living thing within sight. The clown, with his barrel-jumping antics and funny dances, created a diversion to bait the bull away from the downed rider. Sam made light of his job, but it was obviously a pretty dangerous one, and even a seasoned clown was not immune from being crippled.

Charlie and Sam traded some stories, downed some coffee, had a couple of laughs. He was a nice fella, good-natured. Booted feet resting on the lower rung of the fence, the two men watched Rollie Hawkins do warm-ups with his horse, all the while taking several sips from a hip flask.

"He's going at it pretty early, isn't he?" Charlie commented.

"That he is."

"He gonna be all right to ride today?"

Sam shrugged. "Not for me to say. I assume there are folks who look out for that kind of thing."

"I sure hope so. A red-eyed bull and a pie-eyed rider don't usually mix."

Sam laughed. "Well put, my friend." He removed his booted foot from the fence rung. "Well, it's about that time to get going. Good luck out there."

"Same to you, Sam. Don't get in the way of any horns, now, hear?"

They shook hands, and Sam went off to tend to his job.

Charlie had a while to go yet before his events. His gaze roamed the stands, as it had been doing for the past hour, looking for Cassie. Just as he'd decided she wasn't there, a waving hand out of the corner of his eye caught his attention. Yep, there they were, mother and daughter, just settling in about a third of the way up. He got a nice soaring feeling in his chest at the sight. He waved back.

The bleachers were filled with shouting, enthusiastic spectators, but Cassie and Trish managed to find two seats just in from the aisle, next to an extremely pregnant woman with a two-year-old in tow. Cassie didn't envy her at all. Not only was it horribly uncomfortable to be pregnant in summer, but the towheaded little boy was obviously a handful, squirming on his mother's lap, trying to get down, complaining, never being still for a moment. Trish, who was naturally maternal, took the little boy in hand, playing with him and telling him stories.

Cassie smiled at the pregnant woman. "Terrible twos?"

"Terrible twos since the day he was born," the woman said and expelled a huge sigh. "Used to be able to keep up with him, but you know how it is." She patted her stomach. "I have to heave a whole lot of extra weight around nowadays."

"Yes," Cassie said with a smile. "How well I remember."

"Well now, hello there, lovely ladies."

"Charlie!" Trish looked up from playing patty-cake with her little friend to see her hero. She made sure the child was firmly back in his mother's care, then raised her arms to Charlie for a hug. Still standing in the aisle, Charlie picked her up, obliged with a large hug, then set her down.

"How about one for you, too?" he asked Cassie, one eyebrow raised. "I got a lot of hugs to spare today."

She maneuvered her way into the aisle and was quickly enfolded in his arms. It felt as good and as comforting as always, yet there was also an added dimension of melancholy deep inside her. It had taken hold of her the evening before at Trish's bedtime and had refused to release her, and it was a signal that their time together was limited and she'd better prepare herself for loss.

She hugged him tightly, and he must have felt her emotion, because he pulled back, tipped her chin up with his finger, and said, "Come on now, Cassie. What's wrong?"

"I'm worried about you. What if you get hurt today?"

"No need for fussing. I know what I'm doing. It

can look a little rough down there, but I'm protected." He favored her with one of his huge grins, the one that made all the lines at the corner of his eyes crinkle and caused his turquoise-colored eyes to light up like new sunshine. "Heck, ma'am, we cowboys have calluses in places you can't even imagine." He wiggled both eyebrows at her, making her laugh, as he'd intended to do.

He was invited to sit down by the pregnant woman, whose name was Margaret, and as long as he held Trish on one knee and the little boy—Junior was what he was called—on the other, there was enough room.

Together they watched the first event, the trick riding. At the end of that contest, Trish said, "Are you next?"

"Not yet," he told her.

The little boy squirmed some, but after a bit, settled back against Charlie's chest and fell asleep. His mother mouthed her thanks at him, then turned her attention on the arena.

The trick roping was next, which was a lot of fun.

"Now?" Trish asked him when it was over.

"Nope," Charlie said.

"But when?"

"Soon."

When the steer wrestling began, Trish angled her head around to face him, her mouth set in a stubborn line that reminded him so much of her mother, he had to keep himself from smiling at her obvious indignation.

"Charlie?" she said in a loud whisper, obviously conscious of not waking the sleeping little boy on Charlie's other knee. "Are you *ever* going to go down there?"

"Yup, but not till one of my events is called."

"But why aren't you doing this event?"

"Don't have my own horse, darlin'. Felicity is back home, stuffing himself on new hay, more than likely."

"Oh. But I told all my friends to watch for you. They're here with their families. You *are* going to be in the rodeo, aren't you?"

"Sure am, little lady."

He glanced over at Cassie to see her scribbling furiously on a small pad. "What are you doing over there?"

"Taking notes. I intend to use all this—" she waved a hand over the entire arena "—as background in a story or two."

He grinned. "Then make sure you put in there how Cowboy Charlie sat his horse and rode that bull with the best of them. And how he won a whole bunch of money, too. Felicity'll be in there, too, won't he?"

"Needless to say. But tell me, how are you judged? Isn't it about how long you stay on the horse?"

"Yes, but there's both skill and luck involved. For instance, you need to draw a good bucker—that's a horse who's mean enough—then stay on it, if you want to impress the judges." He grinned. "Nobody gets credit for riding a rocking-chair horse. So, it's a gamble whether you go home broke, loaded down with prize money or on a stretcher."

Cassie shivered. "I wish you hadn't said that."

"Hey, not me, darlin'." He leaned in and whispered in her ear. "I promise."

The little boy began to fuss, so Margaret took him onto her lap. She pointed to the arena. "There's Daddy," she told him.

Charlie checked to see where she was pointing. "That your husband?" he asked her. "Rollie Hawkins?"

Her huge smile of pride indicated that he was. Charlie thought it was a shame that this nice young woman and child, with another one on the way, too, had a drinker for a husband. They all watched as Rollie did well with the steer he wrestled.

"He's mighty good," Charlie told the woman who, again, smiled her pleasure at the compliment.

Meantime, he noticed that Cassie was still busy making notes in her pad. "Hey, I got one for you to write about," Charlie said. "Trish, you'll enjoy this. We got a contest back home called wild cow milking."

"Wild cow milking?" the little girl repeated.

"Yes. There are these wild herds roaming the plains, and the boys'll capture one of the cows and turn it loose in the pen. One cowboy ropes her while the other runs on foot, carrying a jar, and tries to obtain about an inch of milk in it. If he can do that—and believe you me, it isn't an easy thing to do—he runs to the judges to show it."

Cassie laughed. "That's it! 'Charlie and the Wild Cow Milking Contest,'" she teased.

"Don't you dare. I'd never enter that—it's not fitting with my image."

"And just what image is that?"

"Why, the strong, silent type."

"For a strong, silent type, you sure do tell a lot of stories," she replied sardonically.

"It bother you, my tale telling?"

"Are you kidding? I find you fascinating."

He winked at her, a warm, personal expression in his gaze. "It's mutual."

An *ohh* went up from the crowd as one of the riders slid under the steer and was nearly trampled before he was rescued.

Charlie smoothed his hair and settled his hat firmly on his head. "Well, time to go."

"Now?" Trish said.

He tickled her and she giggled. "Now. Wish me luck."

The little girl kissed his cheek. "Good luck, Charlie. I'm keeping all my fingers crossed for you."

Then Cassie kissed his cheek, too, a light peck that still made his skin tingle.

"I'm set for life, luckwise, now."

"Don't you get hurt, you hear me?" she said, trying for lightness, but with an undertone of seriousness.

"Yes, ma'am." Easing his way past Margaret and Junior, he tipped his hat to them all and took off. He was more than ready for what lay ahead, and had a real good feeling about his chances.

Charlie was competing in three events, the saddle bronc busting, bareback bronc busting and, the final event of the day, riding the bull.

From the sidelines Charlie watched the first two contestants in the saddle bronc event get bucked up and off their mounts pretty quick. He was third, and was hoping he could stay on for the limit, which was ten seconds. He wasn't familiar with any of these horses, so what he'd told Cassie, that luck played as much a part as skill in which horse you drew, was especially true. If you got a sulker or chute-crazy animal, your chances lowered real quick.

He got a sulker, and a real aggravating one at that. After Charlie's borrowed saddle was dropped into place and cinched, he lowered himself onto the beast's back. But when the gate was opened, the horse decided it didn't feel like leaving the chute. Squatting back on his haunches, he refused to move. No amount of cursing, spurring or coaxing was going to make this persnickety animal come out till he was good and ready.

Charlie gritted his teeth with exasperation, seeing the prize money take wing and set off for foreign lands. At that moment the horse decided it was ready, and he took off with a mighty unexpected leap, causing Charlie to break his balance across the saddle's cantle board. Try as he might, he couldn't seem to get his seat back and wound up heading upward to see what the moon was made of. After that, he landed on his rump with a thud.

He got right up, dusted off his seat with his hat, and headed back to the fence, slightly dejected. In all honesty, he doubted anyone could have stayed on that bronc, but that didn't help. Luck hadn't been with him on this one; he could only hope the other two events would prove luckier.

Rollie was next up after Charlie, and he got a real spirited horse. Despite his drinking, he managed to stay on the critter for the full ten seconds. The crowd cheered their hometown boy, and he waved his hat at them with a lopsided grin. Charlie nodded. The man was good, real good, there was no getting around it.

In the stands Cassie had watched, a scream stuck in her throat as Charlie took a header. Only when he got right back up and walked off, without a limp or any obvious evidence of spurting blood, did she understand what he had meant. It might look violent and dangerous, but if you were skilled, you were probably going to be okay. *Probably,* she thought darkly, being the operative word here.

But what about the time when he wasn't okay, when his skill failed and he got injured? From what she could tell, it was all too possible for a serious injury, even death, to occur. She shuddered. Men and their capacity—no, their *need*—for the rough side of life, the urge to compete, the violence. Even though Charlie was mostly gentle in his attitudes, he was all man. He had that temper, that insistence on meeting physical challenges.

Again she shuddered. Good Lord, he was going to do this, make her heart stop, in two more contests, and she hoped she could tolerate it.

Trish seemed utterly unfazed by the whole thing. It must have seemed like a big cartoon—men getting thrown off and bouncing right back up to the cheers of an adoring crowd. Cassie wondered at what age she'd realize it wasn't a cartoon, and wished she could spare her daughter that day.

Charlie's next event was the bareback bronco ride and he did a little better this time. Cassie held her hand over her mouth so as not to scream in terror and frighten Trish, but, oh, it was difficult. He came out of the chute on what looked to her like an extremely crazed animal. Its eyes were wild, and its strong back legs kicked in the air, while it charged forward, head down, back arched in an attempt to unseat Charlie.

All the man had to hold on to was one little strap, and did he bounce up and down! Lord, she thought, how did the body take that kind of punishment and come out in one piece?

Charlie was pleased to have lasted his ten seconds, but didn't feel it had been a sterling performance. After his turn he watched the others compete. Rollie got himself a chute-crazy bronc this time, one who was not in the mood for a contest that day. That animal reared, backed, fought and kicked till he wore himself down, and all of this before he left the chute. By the time he came out into the arena, he was moping along, plum wore-out. For Rollie, luck of the draw had gone the other way this time.

But another local, a boy from a nearby ranch who Charlie had nodded to in the Burger Barn a couple of times that week, did real well on his mount. In bareback, the judges marked you on how you rode, how you spurred your horse and how rough the horse was in the first place. This boy did well on all counts, and Charlie figured he'd win; as for himself, he'd be lucky to place in the top four.

Which left his last chance. The bull. He clenched his jaw with determination. If he wanted to get any prize money today, have any chance of helping Cassie achieve her dream, it would have to be the bull or nothing.

Bull riding, Charlie knew from experience, was one of the most sensational events in any rodeo. There was always that chill of expecting to see a man thrown, tromped, gored or tossed on the horns of a mad bull. A rider had to stay on for eight seconds from the time the bull left the chute, which might not sound like a long time, but it was mighty long when on the back of a whirling bull. You had to keep one hand on the rope, the other up in the air at all times.

The bulls used were Brahmas, which had been crossbred and had all the bad qualities of their ancestors and none of the good. Heavy and loose skinned, with a huge hump on his shoulders and lethally sharp hoofs, a Brahma looked like a nightmare come to life. His nature wasn't a pleasant one in the first place, but it wasn't helped by the strap that was tightened across its genitals just before the chute was opened; as soon as he came out of the chute, he began a crazed, spinning jump and kept up this tight spin till the rider was thrown.

Charlie's turn was near the end, but he spent the time talking to himself, gearing up to ride that bull. Rollie went before him, and this time the liquor he'd been sipping all day finally caught up with him. To the cheers of all, he actually managed to stay on for about two seconds, but he was thrown off with a mighty heave and lay on the ground unconscious—or passed out from alcohol. Either way, he wasn't getting up.

Sam the clown showed up right away to ease the angry animal away from Rollie, and most of the crowd's concentration was focused on that drama—you could hear the group holding its breath as one.

Not Charlie. His attention was caught by the sight of a towheaded little boy who had somehow managed, undetected, to crawl under the fence and was now toddling into the center of the ring. It was Rollie's child, the one who'd sat on Charlie's lap up in the stands, and now he was rushing on fat little legs, his arms held out, yelling "Daddy! Daddy fall down!"

Without thinking, Charlie leaped the fence and dashed into the arena where the bull's attention had been distracted away from Rollie and the clown and onto the small newcomer making all the noise. Running as fast as he could, Charlie scooped up the little boy and, his heart all the way up in his throat with fear, headed for the nearest fence, the bull hot on his heels.

He managed to toss the child into the arms of a waiting cowboy on the other side of the fence, and had one boot on the lower rung, preparatory to heaving himself over, when the bull caught up to him. In an instant he felt the sharp stab of the bull's horn in his back, heard his shirt rip and could almost smell the blood flowing out from the wound. Before the beast could attack again, Charlie managed to scramble over the top—with the help of a lot of arms—and onto the ground on the other side.

The pain was unlike any he'd ever felt before, and he went in and out of consciousness for a few moments. In the background he heard people asking if he was okay, listened to the crowd's sigh of relief as, apparently, all were now safe from the bull. This was followed by cheers for the next rider, who came out of the chute as if nothing unusual had happened, followed quickly by groans as he apparently bit the dust. It goes on, business as usual, Charlie thought.

Then he stopped noticing anything at all.

He awoke again in the medical tent, lying on his side on a cot, his entire body, but especially his back, racked with pain. At first he was disoriented, but all too soon he knew just where he was and just what had happened. He'd messed up, but good. The registration fee had gone for nothing. He was not going to ride the bull, not today, for sure, which meant he was not about to win any prize money.

But there was more to regret: as gambling was legal

in Nevada, he'd placed some side bets. As a newcomer, his odds of winning had been nigh on to impossible, so he'd figured to clean up, big-time, which would have meant a whole lot more than prize money, all for Cassie.

But he hadn't won a thing, not a plugged nickel. Charlie was now as penniless as he'd been when Cassie had wished him real and he'd landed on her porch.

He groaned; the pain was pretty awful. A bearded man in a Stetson came around from behind him and stood looking down on him.

"I've got the wound cleaned out," he told him, his face solemn, "but I'm going to give you something more for the pain before I start stitching you up." Without a warning, Charlie felt a new sharp pain as the doc stuck him with a needle. It all happened so quickly, Charlie didn't have any time to ask what in tarnation the man thought he was doing, or even to protest.

By the time Cassie got there he was feeling drowsy, and the acute discomfort was fast receding. Her face as she gazed down on him was a portrait of alarm—huge eyes, pale skin, biting her bottom lip as though trying to take off a layer of skin.

"Charlie? Are you okay?"

"Excuse me," the doc said from behind him. "You'll have to wait outside till I finish up here."

She put her hand on her throat. "But, is he going to be all right?"

"I'm working on it."

She began to back away, but Charlie muttered "Wait," so she stopped. "One minute, doc, okay?" He was hoarse, and it was hard to get the words out.

"Half a minute. That bleeding's about to start up again."

Charlie motioned for Cassie to come closer. When she got there, she had to bend over his still form to hear him.

"I'm sorry," he whispered.

"For what?" She settled on her haunches so he could meet her eyes.

"I'm sorry," he said again. "Cowboy Charlie didn't come through, did he?" He stopped, swallowed. Speaking was real difficult, but he had to get this out. "All I wanted to do was gather up my prize money and...march into the bank tomorrow—" he took a shallow breath, which was about all he could manage "—and pay off a year of mortgages for you. All I wanted...was to leave you with some sense of security." His breath came in short pants now. "I wanted to— Oh, Cassie, darlin', I was supposed to rescue you."

Cassie shook her head, the fear gone from her eyes and disbelief taking its place. "Instead you rescued a child who was about to get gored to death! What's the matter with you? You're sorry? You're a hero."

He almost smiled at her fierce defense of him. "But not your hero," he whispered.

Cassie felt herself losing it then. What was wrong with this man? Her temper snapped and she let him have it, both barrels. "Will you stop saying that? I don't need you to be my hero, I need you to be all right!" She took his hand, squeezed it as hard as she could. "I'll be fine, I promise, and so will Trish. We're healthy, I have a job, life is not a terrible burden. If I lose the house, we'll get an apartment. We won't starve. In the scheme of things, with all the poverty and war in the world, we're doing pretty damned well." She felt tears filling her eyes, and she put her hand over her mouth and choked back a sob. "Now, please Charlie, *please*. Just get better."

His eyelids fluttered, then closed. She looked up at the doctor, her worry now escalated to fever pitch. "He will get better, won't he?"

"That's what I'm about to find out."

Not an answer in the least, but she imagined it was all he knew. She rose, backed away. "Well then, I'd better get out of your way." She stopped. "Charlie?" she said one last time.

But he was already unconscious, hopefully from the medication and not some kind of internal head injury.

"I love you," she whispered into the air, then left before she broke down completely in front of the doctor.

As she walked out of the tent, the Fourth of July fireworks were in full gear. Brilliant colors and shapes filled the air above her, accompanied by popping noises and the crowd's cheers of approval. Trish was with one of her friends' families, and Cassie needed to find her and tell her that Charlie was going to be okay...whether that was true or not.

As she hurried along, she mused on the fact that she usually loved this holiday, loved what it represented—freedom, a new start, joy and happiness. But there was no way she could take part in this year's celebration. Her heart was heavy with worry and dread.

Despite her brave words to Charlie, it was hard to summon up anything positive to look forward to. Her heart was heavy with total lack of hope.

Oh, Lord, she thought. Charlie had told her his rules dictated he would be leaving her. Was this the way he would make his exit?

By dying?

Chapter Nine

After opening the front door, Cassie had her hands full, what with helping Charlie into the house as he leaned against her, one arm slung over her shoulder and mumbling under his breath about how no woman ought to be supporting him this way. It was not helped by Trish's constant questions about if Charlie was going to be all right and if the stains on his shirt would come out in the washing machine. Cassie would have thought the sight of blood would horrify her child; instead it seemed to fascinate her.

"Trish," she ordered, as Charlie stumbled on the small rug by the front door and Cassie just managed to keep him upright, "go upstairs and get ready for bed."

"But, Mom," she protested, Charlie's Stetson on her head, covering most of her face. "I want to help you with Charlie."

"You'll help me by getting ready for bed and being as quiet as you can."

"Go on now, Trish," Charlie said, his voice as firm as he could make it. "Listen to your momma. I'll be fine, you wait and see."

"Promise?"

"Cross my heart."

"Can I sleep with your hat tonight?"

"Yep."

"Okay, then." Trish headed up to her bedroom, then stopped and looked back at them briefly. This time Cassie caught a glimpse of worry that bordered on fear in her daughter's eyes, and wondered if the child was, perhaps unconsciously, reliving the night her father died. Cassie certainly was.

There had been a knock on the door around midnight, followed by the policewoman's news. Cassie, too shocked to feel grief, had stayed up all night, dreading the morning and the fact that she'd have to tell her daughter that her beloved father wouldn't be coming home anytime.

When Charlie left, it would devastate Trish one more time—and now she was older and it would be more real. How Cassie wished she could protect her daughter from all of life's blows, take them for her instead. But she couldn't. What she could do, however, was warn her beforehand; she'd have to do that before too much more time went by. What kind of protection she would be able to offer her own heart was another matter altogether.

"I'll be up soon, to kiss you good-night," Cassie called to her daughter as she and her patient made their slow way into the house.

Together they watched Trish scamper up the stairs, then Charlie leaned an elbow against the banister and gazed down on Cassie. "I sure am sorry to be so much trouble," he said, panting from exertion. "I know I weigh a goodly amount, and you're such a little thing."

"I'm stronger than I look. But all this could have been avoided, you know, if you'd let them take you to the hospital."

"I don't want any more strange people poking me again," he said, obviously cranky. "Besides, that needle hurt."

Cassie glared up at him. "The needle hurt? What about being thrown from a horse? What about getting gored by a bull? You mean to tell me that didn't hurt?"

He shrugged. "I'm used to that. I didn't cotton to that needle, no sir."

"You are one strange man." She let out an exasperated sigh then took a firm grip around his waist. "Sling your arm over my shoulder so we can get up these stairs."

"Why the stairs?"

"I'm giving you my bed tonight."

"No, ma'am, you're not," he replied firmly, steering them both away from the stairs and heading for the living room. "The davenport will be just fine."

"But it's not nearly as comfortable, Charlie. And you're too tall."

"I'll be fine. Just help me over there, then you go on your way."

Cassie halted in her tracks, causing Charlie to do the same. "Listen, you. Enough with the strong, silent, brave, Man of the West. The only way they let me take you home was if I promised to attend to you all night, check for fever, give you your antibiotics.

So I will not be getting on my way, I'll be taking care of you."

"What are those anti things?"

"Antibiotics. Pills to keep the infection away."

"Pills. Don't much like pills, either," he grumbled, "or a woman fussing over me."

"We have an expression nowadays. 'Get over it.' Like it or not, you're getting pills for pain and pills for infection. And if you're insisting on the couch, you're getting me sitting nearby in a chair, all night. I'll be fussing as much as you need, so no more complaining." Determined, she led him toward the couch. "It's not open to discussion."

His voice was resigned but faintly amused as he said, "My, my, you surely do have a stubborn nature, don't you?"

"And this is the first time you're discovering that?"

"I suspected."

"Humph."

They reached the old flower-print easy chair adjacent to the couch. "Can you sit here while I make up the couch?"

"Yes," he said, and lowered himself slowly by bracing his hands on the chair's arms.

She could see that it was extremely painful to do so, but the man was nothing if not stoic. The doctor had told her that he'd rarely seen anyone come through what Charlie had gone through without screaming, but he'd gritted his teeth and refused to cry out.

Quickly Cassie found an old plastic tablecloth and spread it over the couch, in case he bled in the night. She covered it with blankets, then a cotton sheet and more blankets. After that, she kneeled next to Charlie's feet and pulled his boots off—not an easy task. After she set them down by the foot of the couch, she went to work getting him up off the chair. It took quite a while, and he grunted but refused to complain.

Men, she thought. Didn't they understand that it felt better to cry the pain out? She supposed they did. But that didn't change their basic nature, which sent signals that complaining was not manly.

Working together, she and Charlie managed to get him onto the couch, lying on his side. She tucked blankets around him, put a pillow under his head, did the best she could to make him comfortable. When he was all set, she was breathing as hard as he was but managed to ask, "Are you in pain?"

"Some," he grunted, in what she supposed was a classic example of cowboy understatement. His eyes were closed, and his mouth was pinched with strain.

She checked her watch. "The next pill's not due for an hour or so. What do you do back home for pain?"

"A whiskey if it's available. Simon Tompkins's rotgut if it's not. Couple of swallows of that stuff, and you don't much care if there's a tornado two feet away. You just lie there nice and peaceful."

"Alcohol is out when you take antibiotics. So you'll have to make do with tea."

His eyes snapped open in horror. "Tea?" His snort was as disdainful as a snort could get. "Tea's what they give sissies."

"Not in all cultures. I'll put lots of honey in it, and you'll like it." She left him, still grousing away about sissy drinks and pushy women.

When she got to the kitchen, she gripped the edge

of the counter, biting her bottom lip to keep from crying out. God, she thought, how much more could she take? The effort of holding back her fear from Charlie had cost her in energy and strength, and she sagged against the tiles.

It was bad enough seeing him thrown from that horse, worse seeing that huge, angry bull head for him and pin him to the fence. But on top of that, she'd almost lost him today. An inch more, up, down or sideways, the doctor had said, and the bull's horn would have pierced either a lung, Charlie's heart, or his kidneys. As luck would have it, the jab had missed all those vital organs.

She let the fear wash over her, shuddered, then pulled herself upright, swallowing back threatening tears. For a woman who rarely cried, she had sure done a lot of it in the week since Charlie had entered her life.

But there was no time for that, not with all the work still left to do. Charlie's wound had put him in danger of infection, and she was to expect fever that night and into the next day. He could like it or not, think of himself as a sissy or not, but who cared? The man was getting hot tea, his brow mopped and pills every four hours.

If he was going to leave her, then it would be to go back to his other life, "back home" as he called it, and not into a hole six feet deep in a cemetery, or to an afterlife that Cassie didn't even know if she believed in.

The first time Charlie came awake that he was aware of, he couldn't seem to open his eyes. Feeling feverish and restless, he tried to kick his blankets away, but it hurt too much. He heard himself mumbling nonsense, then heard Cassie's voice right by his ear, murmuring soothing words. Soon he felt the relief of a cold cloth on his forehead and more of her calm murmuring. Even though he still lacked the strength to open his eyes, her voice had the effect of making him less fidgety.

"Cassie." His mouth felt as parched as a sand pit.

"Hmm?"

"Water."

He tasted the drops the moment she put the glass to his mouth. She helped him angle his head so he could drink. "You're an angel," he told her. He tried to raise his eyelids, but they felt gritty, glued shut.

"Hardly an angel. Take these pills while you're at it."

He made a face but did as she said, then heard her set the glass down.

"Yes," he went on, dizzy and disoriented. "An angel from heaven sent to make my time here in your world easier."

She applied the cool cloth to his forehead once more. Blindly he reached for her wrists, then, with great effort, turned himself so he was lying on his back. Ignoring the searing pain from his wound, he pulled her down on top of him. She struggled against him, but at least his hands were still strong, and she lost the battle.

"Charlie, don't. I'm too heavy."

"You're light as a feather duster."

"And you're delirious. You have fever and—"

"Let me smell you," he said, burying his face in her neck. "You know, you have the damnedest smell."

He felt her chest muscles contract against him as she laughed softly. "Gee, thanks a lot. Every woman wants to know she smells."

"But it's such a nice smell. A heavenly smell from a heavenly angel. Lilacs. And powder. And your hair—ever since I first saw you, I've wanted to smell your hair." Releasing one of her wrists, he moved some of her curls under his nose and inhaled deeply. "Even better than your skin."

His head felt light and he knew he sounded drunk. He probably was delirious, but it felt fine. Again Cassie tried to wiggle off him.

"No, stay," he said, his strength waning now from this minor exertion. He was drifting, drifting, into a dark void that called to him. "You keep me warm. Much better than a blanket," he heard himself murmur, then the blackness took him once again.

Exhausted, Cassie lay on top of Charlie, promising herself she'd get up soon. This had to be bad for his wound, him lying on his back this way. And her extra weight wouldn't help the infection heal.

But, in truth, moving seemed too much of an effort at the moment. She'd been up with him, checking his fever, soothing him, giving him pills, for much of the night. Dawn was still a few hours away, and she had only dozed here and there.

Besides, she thought, her own eyelids closing against her will, Charlie's broad, strong chest made a lovely resting place. She felt so right there, so at home. She would relax here, she decided, just for a minute, she told herself. Or two.

This time Charlie came more fully awake, even though he still didn't seem able to raise his eyelids.

For the moment he had no idea where he was, only that a warm weight was pressing on his chest. He took a little time to sort through the tangle in his brain, then slowly it all came back to him. His failure to win money for Cassie. How he'd looked foolish in front of Trish when he'd been tossed, and then how Cassie'd had to nurse him, had to see him bleeding and in pain.

He was mortified, but not just that, he was baffled, too.

What had gone wrong? How had his plans for winning, which had felt so right, managed to fall through so completely? And more, what was he to do next? Even now, he felt a dawning sense of urgency, the feeling that he'd better get on with his task soon, because time was running out.

But what task? He was plum out of plans. A spurt of indignation shot through him. He was grown-up enough to know that life wasn't fair, but how in tarnation was he to rescue the woman if he couldn't make use of the one skill he knew he possessed?

A long, deep, satisfied sigh made him open his eyes. The source of the sigh brought a smile to his lips. Cassie was the weight pressing down on his chest. Lovely Cassie, with her brown curls tickling his chin, her small hands splayed across his shirt.

She heaved another sigh, mumbled something, then turned her head as though to rest it on the other cheek. Her eyes opened and she found herself looking straight at him. He watched as she came slowly awake. Heavy-lidded brown eyes were sleepy and dazed and concerned at the same time. Her hair was all mussed up, and there was a crease across her cheek from his shirt, but her face was soft and peaceful. It was a face he'd remember for eternity.

She smiled a lazy smile at him, so, of course, he kissed her.

It felt as natural as breathing. Her mouth was soft and inviting, and as he slipped his tongue between her lips, he felt her tongue answering. But slowly, in no hurry, just sampling, and liking the taste. It was a hello kiss, an amazing kiss.

He stroked a finger over her cheek, then broke the kiss by raising her chin so he could meet her gaze. "In case you can't tell, I want you awful bad, Cassie."

Frowning, she seemed to come more fully awake. "We can't. You're not well."

"Oh, darlin'," he said with a chuckle, "I'm about as well as a man can get."

He saw the dawning awareness in her eyes when it occurred to her that the bulge she felt pressing against her midsection was not one of the couch pillows. Her eyes widened, then she blinked rapidly, a rosy color suffusing her face.

"So it seems."

He waited for her to say something, anything, but she just kept looking at him. Which didn't alleviate the tightness in his groin area. Quite the opposite, it made it worse.

He said it again. "I want you."

"And I want you."

Her words were just the ones he'd wanted to hear. But another silence followed. Then, ever so slowly, she nodded. But not in happiness at the prospect of making love with him. She seemed more sorrowful than glad.

"Yes," she told him. "Even if it's just this one time, I want to have that one time to remember."

"Don't be sad, now," he said, his finger tracing a pattern over her upper lip. The sight of Cassie troubled about broke his heart, even as his body was still signaling a pressing need. "And I'm not sure how memorable it'll be," he continued with a rueful grin, wanting to dispel some of the seriousness of the moment. "You may have to do all the work."

She managed an answering grin for him, making her eyes light up mischievously. "I can't think of a job that would give me more pleasure."

He began to pull her closer again, but she said, "Wait. Let me check on Trish first."

It was difficult to leave Charlie, but Cassie knew that the last thing either of them needed was her daughter coming upon them, whatever state they were in.

Quickly she ran upstairs to look in on Trish. She was sound asleep, Charlie's hat held tightly in her grip. Poor baby, Cassie thought. She'd had an exhausting few days, too. Her bedside clock said 5:30. Always an unwilling riser, the child would be asleep for a couple of hours yet.

She closed her door, then went downstairs again, more slowly this time. The brief interruption had made her rethink her decision. Was making love with Charlie, which she'd wanted from the first, a smart thing to do? Or would she regret it forever?

Charlie lay sprawled on the couch, using his elbow to try to raise himself up. It was no good, and he dropped back down with a grunt. His discomfort was obvious from the paleness of his skin and the tight muscles around his mouth. The golden bristles of his beard only emphasized the shadows beneath his eyes.

And even so, the man was more attractive than any male of the species had a right to be. She stood over him, hands on hips and scolded, "What were we thinking of? We can't do this. You're too bruised."

He answered her with a cocky grin. "It only hurts if I try to move. I guess I'm just going to have to lie here, real still, and let you have your way with me."

"Even if it hurts?"

"Even if it cripples me for life." He cocked an eyebrow rakishly, and she had to laugh. "I'm willing to give it a try if you are."

She shook her head at his persistence, but understood that there was no going back now. The decision had already been made, by both of them. For her it had been made ages ago, when she first dreamed him up.

"Well, all right, then, if you think it's okay. I'm not exactly experienced in, shall we say, doing all the work."

"It's not my usual way, either, darlin', so I guess we'll learn as we go along."

She stood facing him, her hands at her side, flustered, but excited, too. His willingness to bear painful discomfort to be with her was more than flattering, she was slightly shocked to discover. It was a turn-on. "How...do you suggest we start?"

He crossed his arms behind his head and used them for a pillow. "Glad you asked. There's something I'd like you to do for me, something I've been dreaming about for a while."

"What?"

He pointed to the foot of the couch. "Would you

mind standing over yonder and taking off your clothes? I won't be able to undress you myself, which I deeply regret, but I've been dying to see your body from the get-go.''

"You...you mean you want me to strip?"

"No, Cassie," he said with a small smile. "Not like that, not like some girlie show. Just remove your clothes, one piece at a time, the way you would if you were undressing for the night. And let me just look at you while you do."

She felt suddenly intensely self-conscious. Shy, too, the way she used to feel in childhood when meeting someone new. Sexually her experience had been limited to one high school boyfriend and then Teddy. She wasn't worldly or sophisticated, and wondered suddenly if she would please him.

Turning her back to him so he wouldn't see her embarrassment, she leaned over and removed her loafers. Glancing over her shoulder, she saw an amused expression on Charlie's face.

"Don't you dare laugh at me," she warned.

"Laughing is the farthest thing from my mind. Besides, this way I get to see your back, and that's got to be as beautiful as your front."

His obvious understanding of her discomfort, his willingness to be light and easy about this, warmed her and made her relax inside. She pulled her T-shirt over her head, shaking her head to free her hair as she did, and dropped the shirt to the floor. She unzipped her jeans and let them fall down around her ankles. Telling herself to take her time, she stepped out of them and kicked them away.

All that was left was her bra and panties, and she silently cursed the fact that she'd worn sensible cotton that day instead of silk. They were tucked away in the bottom of her drawer, and she hadn't put them on since Teddy died.

Once again she chanced a glance over her shoulder. The amusement had left Charlie's face; now he watched her with razor-sharp intensity. His chest rose and fell more rapidly; his nostrils flared slightly.

"You have a perfect bottom," he told her. "Round, just like a woman's bottom ought to be."

"It's too big."

"Nonsense, it's perfect."

His words of praise made her bolder still; taking a deep breath, she slowly turned around and faced him. She watched as he sucked in a breath of his own, and his eyes glazed over. Bolder still, Cassie stood tall and proud before him for several moments.

She spread her hands, found herself smiling with a sultriness she didn't know she possessed. "Is this what you wanted?"

Charlie, usually a talkative man, seemed to be struck speechless. He didn't say a word, just raked her up and down with his hungry gaze. Then he expelled a long breath. "Oh, Cassie." He shook his head with wonder. "Oh my, yes, I want you. You are just about the most beautiful woman I have ever seen."

She felt the flush of pleasure begin at her toes and work its way all the way up to her forehead. "I am not."

"Are, too."

"Stop."

"Can't do that. We've already begun."

Spreading his arms wide, he growled, "Come here. Let me show you how much I want you."

He wanted her? It couldn't be any more than she wanted him. The urge to run over to him, tear the rest of their clothes off, and join her body with his was suddenly so overwhelming that she felt nearly faint.

Instead she walked over to him with slow deliberation, her hips swaying ever so slightly, her breasts—still firm, despite one pregnancy—barely bobbing up and down.

He groaned, which made her smile. She kept her gaze focused on his face, saw him run his tongue over his dry lips, felt full of the power a woman feels when she is the object of male desire. Doubts rose but the joy of the moment rose more, and she wanted to laugh in triumph.

She reached him, leaned over to kiss his mouth...

And the doorbell rang.

Chapter Ten

The first time it sounded she almost didn't hear it over the noise of roaring in her ears and the heavy breathing emanating from both her and Charlie. But then it rang again, annoying, intrusive.

"Ignore it," Charlie said, one hand cupped over her breast, his thumb teasing her taut nipple.

"Can't. It'll wake Trish up."

To the sound of Charlie's muttered curse, Cassie scrambled to the foot of the couch and threw on her clothes. The bell sounded one more time. Raking her fingers through her tousled hair, she hurried to the door.

The morning sun was just rising over the distant mountains as she pulled the door open, keeping the screen door locked. There on the front porch stood three men who looked as though they could have come from Charlie's home, down to plaid shirts, jeans, Stetsons and boots, all well-worn and dust laden.

For a moment Cassie had the absurd notion that they'd come to escort Charlie back to fiction land.

Removing his hat, the older one spoke first. "Sorry to bother you so early in the morning, ma'am."

"Who are you?"

"I'm hoping this is where we can find Charles Culpepper. This is the address he gave."

"Who wants to know?" Her suspicions were growing. Strange as it sounded, maybe Charlie's rules did include a committee to see that he went back to where he belonged.

"My name is Kyle Bartlett." Pointing to a good-looking young man in his late twenties, he said, "This here's Rollie Hawkins and the other one's Sam Milton." The other two nodded and removed their hats, too.

The name Rollie Hawkins rang a bell. A light dawned. These were men who had been at the rodeo yesterday.

"What do you want with Charlie?"

"Please, ma'am," Kyle, obviously the spokesman, continued, "if you'll tell him we need to see him? It's real important."

"He's...not well."

"We know. It's why we're here."

"One moment."

Cassie closed the door, then returned to the living room. While she'd been gone, Charlie had covered himself with a blanket and had somehow managed to prop himself on a couple of pillows, so he was in a semisitting position.

"Who is it?"

"Three men named Kyle and Rollie and Sam. They're insisting on seeing you."

He laughed ruefully, then shook his head. "Their timing could have been a mite better."

"Tell me about it."

"Well, sure, tell them to come on in."

When Cassie escorted the three visitors into the living room, they all stared at him with concern.

"Hi," Charlie said. "You've all met Cassie Nevins?"

They nodded at her, said they were pleased to meet her, then returned their attention to Charlie. "How you doing there?" Sam asked.

"Just fine," Charlie said easily. "Takes more than one ornery bull to put me down. But isn't it kinda early to be paying a social call?"

Again it was Kyle who spoke, and he addressed himself to Cassie. "Sorry to do this so early, Ms. Nevins, but Rollie and me have to get back to our ranches, and Sam here has to catch a plane, so we wanted to take care of this first."

"It's all right," she assured them, "I wasn't asleep."

Charlie couldn't let that one pass, so he said with a sly grin, "Me, neither. Cassie was taking care of me, as a matter of fact. Doing a mighty fine job of it, too."

Cassie shot him a look that would have put a naughty schoolboy in his place, then turned her attention back to the visitors. "May I make you gentlemen some coffee?"

When they all demurred, she said, "Well, sit down, then."

"We'll be leaving right away," Kyle said.

For the first time Rollie spoke up. "Sure glad to see you in one piece," he told Charlie.

He waved away the comment. "Hey, like I said, I'm not ready to be buried yet. How's your boy?"

"Alive." Sudden tears sprang into the young man's eyes, causing the others to avert their gazes. Rollie took out a huge handkerchief from his back pocket and blew his nose. "Thanks to you."

As the others shuffled their feet in embarrassment, Charlie shook his head. "No need, anyone would have done—"

"Yes, thanks to you," Rollie insisted, then blew his nose again forcefully, wiped around his eyes and stuffed the handkerchief back into his rear pocket.

Kyle took over again. "We want you to have this." For the first time, Charlie noticed that Kyle had been holding a large manila envelope, which he now handed to him.

Frowning, Charlie looked at it, then back up at Kyle. "What is it?"

"All the winnings from yesterday. Everyone threw in his share, because of what you did for little Rollie, Jr."

"Some of the entrance fees are in there, too," Sam put in, "although they didn't have to. Folks just wanted to. And there's extra, too, whatever else anyone wanted to throw into the pot, just to say thank you. Rollie's a pretty popular figure, you know."

The tears in Rollie's eyes had still not dried completely. "What you did changed my life."

Charlie found himself uncomfortable with all this emotion from the young cowboy. Of course, in his experience, men who liked the bottle overly much tended to such displays of sentimentality. Out of nowhere he was struck again with that feeling that had been growing since yesterday, a sense that he was...fading away.

That time was running out.

Rollie was still talking. "Yes, you changed my life," he repeated. "I'm off the sauce for good. I took the vow this morning, with these gentlemen as my witnesses." The others nodded solemnly.

"Well, good," Charlie said, distracted. His body felt strange, as though he were only partly in it anymore.

Rollie went on, sincerity shining with every word. "I almost lost my little boy, and if I had, I would have wanted to die, too. See, if I hadn't been drinking, I'd have seen him there. He always likes to get close when I ride, and my wife, she looked away for a minute and there he was, scampering down the stairs, and, Lord, I can't think about it." He lowered his head in shame.

Charlie, embarrassed for the man, diverted everyone's attention by holding the envelope up in the air. "Well, this is sure nice of all of you, but I can't take this."

"Sure you can," Kyle said.

"No. I didn't earn it fair and square."

Sam spoke up again. "You did, too. You earned it in more ways than one. I watched you, and you're a real rodeo man, you know what you're doing. If you'd been able to ride the bull, maybe you'd have won that and more. See?"

"But Rollie there's a lot better rider than I am—"

As though Charlie hadn't spoken, Sam plowed right on. "And if you save a life," he insisted, "there should be some kind of reward. It's only fitting."

"Yes, but—"

"Charlie," Cassie said for the first time, sensing an argument brewing and wanting to defuse it. "I have a feeling that if you don't take the money, these men will be insulted."

Three heads nodded in unison. "That's right," Sam said.

"Insulted?" Charlie echoed, his eyebrows raised in surprise. "Truly?"

"Truly," Rollie managed.

Kyle added, "We insist."

Cassie held her breath. The aura of testosterone meeting testosterone filled the room with a powerful, distinctly male tension, and she wanted it to stop.

"Well," Charlie said reluctantly. "All right, then."

Whew, she thought. War averted, one more time.

"Sure I can't offer you gentlemen some coffee?" she said brightly. "Toast?"

Kyle took over again. "No, ma'am, we have to get going, like I said. Ranch work begins at dawn. Well, goodbye, Charlie." They all put their hats back on, then one by one, tugged the edges at Cassie. "Nice meeting you."

Rollie smiled at Charlie. "You take care, now. And if you're ever this way again, let's see who can stay on that bull the longest."

"I might just take you up on that," he replied.

Cassie walked them to the door, watched as they all got into an old pickup truck and took off. The sun was fully visible now, casting a bright glow over the morning. It was going to be another hot day, typical for July. And, as the holiday was over, she'd have to go back to work. Back to her regular life.

When she returned to her living room, Charlie was frowning at the envelope. "It just doesn't feel right."

"Tough," she said with a smile. "How much do you think is in there?"

"I have no idea. Would you mind counting it?"

She took the envelope and peeked inside. On top there were lots of crumpled bills, mostly fives and some ones. "Looks like a couple of hundred, at least. I'll count it at the kitchen table."

"First," Charlie said, "come here." He patted the sofa next to him.

She sat down and he took her face in his hands and kissed her. It was a sweet kiss, filled with a tender longing, and she returned it. But the melancholy feeling was back, invading her every pore.

Charlie gazed deeply into her eyes. "I sure am sorry we were interrupted."

"Maybe it was for the best," she said, biting her lower lip.

"Really?"

"I don't know. I'm going to count your money."

Some time later, when Charlie hadn't heard from Cassie for a while, he managed to make his way into the kitchen. She was there, sitting at the table and staring at what was on it. Spread out all over the surface were a series of bills in piles. Her face registered shock and disbelief.

"What's going on here?" He leaned against the doorway for support.

She looked up at him, as though awakened from a dream. "I can't believe it. Do you have any idea what's here?"

"I surely don't."

"How does $7,158.32 sound?"

It was his turn to get still. "Like a whole lot of

money," he said quietly, as all the pieces fell into place.

She shook herself, then scolded, "You shouldn't be up."

"Had to use your bathroom. Seven thousand, you say?"

"And $158 and change."

He nodded. Yes, of course. It all was clear now, which was why he felt so calm. "Well, now." He nodded again. "I guess this is the way it was supposed to happen."

"The way what was supposed to happen?"

He made his way over to the table and lowered himself onto the chair across from her. His body ached from the effort, but it didn't matter anymore. He riffled through one of the piles. "This is your money."

"No it's not. It's yours."

"No, darlin'. This was my reward money and that goes to you. Remember? I'm here to help you with the mortgage. It was what you asked for that first day, and now I'm giving it to you, the way I'm supposed to. And," he added with a small smile, "if you don't take it, I'll be insulted."

At her own words being thrown back at her, she too smiled. "Well, maybe some of it."

"All of it. See? I didn't earn it at the rodeo. I earned it by saving someone, the way you always have me do in your stories. It make sense."

There was a long silence in the room as they gazed at each other, unspoken messages passing between them like electricity through wires.

Finally Charlie spoke again. "As soon as the bank opens, we're marching in there to your Mr. Moffit and plunking this money down. I want to get a look at his face when he understands there will be no foreclosure anytime soon. You and Trish will still have your house."

As though the mention of her name had magical consequences, Trish took that moment to appear in the doorway, still clutching Charlie's Stetson and rubbing her eyes sleepily. "Mommy?" She stared at the table. "Mommy? What's all that?"

"Play money."

"It sure looks real."

"I guess it's real, then." But Cassie felt as though she were anything but real, in a dream state, and she wasn't sure if she wanted to wake up or not. She opened her arms. "Come here, honey, and say good morning."

The little girl walked over to her mother and put her arms around her neck. "Charlie," she said, "the back of your shirt is still yucky."

He nodded. "I know."

Cassie gazed at him over Trish's head. "Before the bank, we take you to the doctor to get your bandage changed."

"I don't think that will be necessary."

"And why not?"

"Because I won't be here much longer."

Trish's head snapped up from her mother's shoulder. "What do you mean? Are you going away?"

He rose from the chair and knelt down in front of the little girl. "I have to go, darlin'. It's time."

The child's eyes filled with tears, and his heart turned over for the pain he was causing her.

"But why?"

He stroked her baby-soft cheek with the back of

his hand, feeling the salt tears on his skin. "Because I was only real for a little while. Now I have to get back home."

"But—" She couldn't go on, just burst into sobs. He hugged her, wincing some from the effort. But even the pain wasn't as bad now. His body wasn't whole anymore, and he wondered if soon he would be like a ghost, his outline visible but the rest of him see-through, like thin paper.

As he patted Trish's head, he gazed at Cassie. The look of grief on her face wrenched his heart something fierce. But he had so much still to do, and so little time left to do it in.

"I want you to have my hat," he told Trish.

She lifted her head, huge eyes, just like her mother's but a little lighter, filled with tears. "Really?"

"Yes. So you'll always remember me."

"But—" She sniffled, tried to stop crying. "But will I ever see you again?"

"I don't know. You just might. It's not up to me."

"Who is it up to?"

"I wish I knew."

"But I don't want you to go." This brought on a fresh onslaught of tears.

"I'll still be here, in the stories your momma tells you. And in your memories. Just not like this, not real. Tell you what, though."

Trish sniffled some more, wiped her hand under her nose. "What?"

"You're going to have ballet lessons now."

"I am?" Even with her eyes glowing with moisture, the look on her face was surprised. She turned toward her mother. "Can I, Mommy?"

"You bet. It's Charlie's goodbye present to you."

The child turned to face him again. "I'd rather have you stay."

"And I'd rather stay. But you'll make me real happy if you get those lessons and do real good. Okay?"

She didn't answer, just laid her head on his shoulder.

They sat outside the bank in her car and held each other's hands tightly. Cassie was dressed for work and, except for his shirt and Stetson, Charlie wore the outfit he'd shown up in a week ago, down to the spurs on his boots and the six-guns in their holster.

"Go now," he told her.

"Aren't you coming in?"

"There isn't time."

She paused, taking this in. "Oh. When I come out you'll be gone, won't you." It wasn't a question.

"I'm pretty sure. I can feel myself fading more and more."

"Oh, Charlie."

No, she would not cry. There had been enough tears, hers and Trish's and even a few from Charlie that morning. Biting her bottom lip, she held on to his hands even tighter. Maybe she could keep him here through the sheer force of her need for him. "What if I don't go in there? What if I don't give them the money? What if I tear it all up right now?"

"It doesn't matter." His tone was even, a little remote sounding. "I've done my part, and so I have to go back." He untied the large kerchief he wore around his neck and handed it to her. "Trish got the hat, so this is all I have to give you. Will you take it?"

She fingered it lovingly. "Of course."

"You'll need to wash it in that big machine of yours. It's got years of grit on it."

"I'll never wash it. It's your grit, and I love it."

"Do you love me?"

She threw her arms around his neck. "Oh, God. Of course I do."

"I just wanted to hear the words."

"I love you, I love you, I love you."

"And I love you." He pulled her hands away from around his neck. "Go now."

She grasped the handle, then turned back to him, her eyes bright with tears. "Your back. Will it heal okay?"

"That'll be up to you."

"Me?"

"Yep. You write my back injury the way you want it to heal. Maybe you can give me a scar or two. And when you write it, that's how I'll be. Go, darlin', please. Now."

"Will we ever meet again?" She knew she sounded as lost and as young as Trish had when she'd asked the question earlier, but she couldn't help herself.

"I don't know, Cassie. I don't know about the rules."

"I hate your rules," she said with anger.

"They're what brought me here in the first place." He put a finger under her chin and lifted her head so she could meet his gaze. "Are you sorry we met?"

"No. But I'm not going to give up hope that we'll meet again, that we'll be together sometime."

"Then maybe that will be enough."

"Will you remember me?"

"I'll never forget you, not as long as I live."

"You're going to live forever, then," she said fiercely. "I'll just keep writing about you."

"Eternal life," he said with a smile. "Sounds fine. Go now." He stroked her cheek. "You have a child to raise and dreams to make real. Go," he said for the last time. "I love you."

"And I love you."

Choking back a sob, Cassie tore open the door of the car and, brushing past the others on the street, went into the bank, deposited the cash in her checking account, wrote out a check for the next three months' mortgage and left it on Moffit's desk.

The whole time she felt as though she was a machine, doing the next thing in front of her, taking care of what needed to be done. But her heart wasn't with her in that bank, it was outside with the man she'd left sitting in her car.

Maybe, she allowed herself to hope, maybe he'd still be there when she got outside. Maybe the rules could be circumvented, changed. Slowly she pushed open the glass doors and stepped outside. There was still bright sunlight. Still people passing on the street, cars going by.

But Cowboy Charlie was gone.

Weeks later, Cassie was at home, her feet up on her desk, her mind lost in thought when the phone rang. Its jangle made her jump. "Hello," she said into the receiver, not graciously.

"Is this Cassie Nevins?" It was a mature male voice.

"Speaking. Are you selling something?"

"No, but we're buying."

"Excuse me?"

"My name is Donald Albright, and I'm with KidLit Books. You may have heard of us, we're one of the top children's literature publishers in the United States."

"Yes, I've heard of you."

"We'd like to buy your Cowboy Charlie stories."

"My what?" Cassie lowered her feet to the carpet and gripped the edge of her chair.

"We received your Cowboy Charlie stories over a month ago, and we'd like to offer you a contract."

Her head was spinning. "But...how did you get them?"

"Your representative, a Mr. Charles Culpepper, sent them in and asked us to look at them. I assume he's acting as your agent. Would you rather I contacted him?"

"Uh, no, no, it's all right, you can talk to me."

Charlie? Charlie had sent her stories in?

Albright was chuckling now. "It's interesting how this whole thing happened, you know, because most unsolicited manuscripts are tossed into a pile for a reader to peruse, but somehow, yours got to the In basket of one of our senior editors...."

He went on, a chatty man, pleased to be telling her the whole story, but all she heard was that they wanted to buy her work! And that somehow, in the week he'd been here, Charlie had sent them in!

But when? And how?

In the two months since Charlie had left them, Cassie and Trish had existed, but barely, despite the ease of financial pressure. Her child took ballet lessons, went to school, played with her friends. Cassie had enrolled in that art course, worked on her stories, gone to work, cooked dinner. But mother and daughter remained deeply scarred by their loss.

Cassie had tried to explain to Trish what had happened and why Charlie had had to leave, but she didn't have the vocabulary a seven-year-old required to understand it. Lately Trish had stopped talking about him, but she slept with his hat each night.

For herself, Cassie lay awake more nights than she cared to count, and when she slept, dreamed of Charlie. Once she'd even tried rubbing the glasses again, wishing hard for his return, but he must have been right: they only worked once. That once had produced a miracle. A short-lived one, but a miracle nevertheless.

The man on the phone went on to tell Cassie he'd like to meet her, to see any other stories she might have, and how soon could she come to New York, at KidLit's expense, of course, to discuss it?

"As soon as you want me," she told him. "And I'll be bringing my daughter." Buoyed by this startling news, Cassie hoped that this trip would help both of them snap out of their funk.

Cassie slammed the car door and started the engine. She was in a hurry to get to FedEx in the next town over, before the last delivery. In the months since she and Trish had gone to New York, she'd deposited her advance, quit her job and had been writing and drawing up a storm. The stories just kept coming from somewhere in her head, and they were better and better all the time.

Yesterday she'd begun one that was going to be a

full-length book. In a burst of creative energy that felt like nothing she'd ever experienced before, she'd been up all night and most of the day writing the outline. Just an hour ago she'd discussed it with Don on the phone, and he was also enthused, insisted on seeing it right away. She still didn't have a fax machine, so she'd told him she would have it to him by Monday morning.

The book was going to be about the day Cowboy Charlie became real. Not just temporarily real, but forever real. About how he came into the life of a lonely widow and her child and joined their family. And about how he brought them joy and love and happiness.

It was blatant wish fulfillment; Cassie knew it and didn't care. She *had* to write it, felt driven, as though by unseen forces, to get the words on paper. She resented, in fact, having to take this break to mail it out, but she would return right away and continue work. Trish was away at Snow Play camp for the weekend, so her time was her own and she intended to use it fully.

She tore out of her driveway and barreled down the street, onto the highway. It was December, and there was a nip in the high desert air. She felt lighter, more hopeful than she had in months. She hummed as she drove.

Just as she was approaching a cattle-crossing stop sign, a car came from the opposite direction, driven by a teenager, loud music blasting from the open window. The boy was laughing. Suddenly he seemed to lose control, crossed over into her lane, heading straight for her. She swerved quickly to avoid a crash, and wound up plowing into a fence. The impact was strong, but her seat belt held, and although she was thrown forward, she remained in her seat.

The other car didn't stop to see if she was okay; it just continued on its way, the bass-heavy music disappearing into the distance.

Her car shuddered, then came to a stop, the engine stalled. Cassie, dazed and disoriented, sat still, trying to get her bearings. Her heart raced and she felt the pulse pounding in her head. She closed her eyes to stop the spinning sensation. In the back of her mind she realized she'd just had a narrow escape with death, and said a silent prayer of gratitude.

A tapping on her window made her open her eyes. She turned to see who it was.

A man's face appeared, concern etched on it. He tapped again, indicating that she should roll down her window. The man wore a Stetson, had shaggy blond hair, a tan face and turquoise eyes with lines radiating out from the sides.

Cassie's heart stopped, simply stopped. And time stood still.

"Charlie?"

She had to be dreaming. But if she was, then it was the dream she'd been having every night for six months. "Charlie?" she said again, and rolled down her window.

"Excuse me," the man said in Charlie's voice. "Are you all right?"

"Charlie?" she said again, not sure she could say anything else.

He frowned. "How do you know my name?"

"Is that your name?"

"Yes. But tell me, are you hurt?"

Now she heard the slight difference in the voice: it

was Charlie's timbre, but this man sounded more educated, less rural than urban.

She shook her head. "I don't think so."

"Can you move? Get out of the car?"

"Yes, I think I can."

He opened her door and she got out. But her legs were wobbly and she fell against him. He caught her before she fell. "Sure you're all right?" he asked, his strong hands grasping her upper arms, holding her up.

She had to crane her neck to look up at him, and when their eyes met, his quick indrawn breath was audible. He stared at her, the strangest look on his face.

"Hello, Charlie," she said softly, almost afraid to speak.

His hands tightened on her arms. "How do you know my name?"

"Is it Charlie?"

"Yes. Charles, actually."

"I see."

"You didn't answer my question."

"I'm sorry. I don't know that I can."

Another long pause went by. Cassie searched his gaze for signs of recognition, but all she saw was confusion. No, there was something more there, something in back of the confusion, the look of someone trying to remember something he didn't even know he'd forgotten. As though suddenly aware he was holding her arms too tightly, he let her go, his hands dropping to his sides.

"I'm Cassie Nevins," she said, leaning weakly against her car door, "and I thank you for coming to my rescue."

He smiled at her then, a beloved, familiar smile that

lit up his eyes from within. "Charles McMasters. Dr. Charles McMasters. I'm a veterinarian." He pointed to a nearby truck that pulled a horse trailer behind it. "I try to rescue at least one damsel a day, but she usually has four legs."

She smiled back at him and nodded. "A veterinarian. Yes, that makes sense." She didn't explain her remark to him, couldn't really. But it didn't matter, because she *knew*.

Charlie had come back! Not as a cowboy, but as a man who tended animals, a man who could fit in, who could live in her time and her world and be content.

He pushed his hat back and scratched his head, in a dear, familiar gesture that made her heart turn over. "You're going to think me crazy," he said slowly, "but have we met before?"

She licked her dry mouth, almost giddy with excitement. "I don't quite know how to answer that," she said truthfully, holding her breath.

"Oh, I see. Actually, I don't see." The look of puzzlement on his face changed to one of wonder. "Please don't think me forward...but I can't shake the feeling, not that we've met before, but that I...I dreamed you. And now you're real."

"Yes," she said, joy leaping into her heart and filling all the empty places Cowboy Charlie had left. "I had the very same dream."

Epilogue

One year later

There was a good turnout for the book signing today, which made Doc happy for Cassie, as did the fact that it was taking place close to home, in Reno. That meant he and Trish could be here with her. Cassie had been traveling quite a bit in the past month, but now she was at the end of her book tour, and he expelled a sigh of relief. Although Doc understood the public relations demands of a full-time author, he wanted his wife with him in the flesh, not at the end of some long distance wire.

As though she could read his mind, Cassie looked up and blew a kiss to Doc, who stood a few feet away on the sidelines, and then another to Trish, who held his hand tightly.

"Hi, Mommy," Trish said with a small wave of her free hand, then looked up at him, pride dancing in her eyes. He saw other expressions on the child's face—contentment and trust. She had a daddy now, a real one, and she wasn't about to let him go. Over the past year, he and Trish had bonded. It was his first experience with fatherhood, but the little girl made it easy.

As Cassie had explained on that first evening, when she and Doc couldn't stop talking, when there didn't seem to be enough words in the universe to say all they had to say, her daughter had had some pretty bad experiences with men leaving.

Trish had begun by calling him Charlie, but he soon told her he preferred Doc. Doc it was, for quite a few months, then, just a few weeks ago, he'd graduated to Daddy. He liked that. He liked that a lot. He knew that real, deep down trust would take a while. She would need more time to heal fully, but then, anything worthwhile took time.

It had taken time to find Cassie, hadn't it? All his life, in fact. He passed through that life, he'd come to realize, with what he could only describe as a hole in the middle of his soul. An important piece of himself had been missing and, at some deep level, he'd always known it. He'd just assumed that he wasn't a man who was capable of true joy or strong feelings of love, of deep emotions at all.

He'd had a perfectly decent childhood as the only son of stoic, aging parents, Iowa farmers who'd worked their precious few acres every day of their lives. There'd been enough food on the table, even if they'd never been well-off. Doc had had a normal childhood—some friends, a lot of time spent on either a bike or a horse. He'd been a good student, but had always felt a close affinity with animals, so he'd planned on staying on the farm. His folks had surprised him by requesting he go on to college, to be the first one in the family to do so. They'd asked so little of him, so he'd agreed, eventually getting his degree in veterinary medicine.

Along the way, there had been relationships with women, but none of them long lasting. In each affair, that crucial element—that ability to surrender his heart to anyone one hundred percent—had been glaring in its absence.

Shortly after he became accredited, Doc's parents had died, one month after the other. He'd always yearned to live surrounded by mountains instead of flat plains, so he'd sold the farm and, up until a year ago, had a small ranch and a veterinarian practice in Montana. He'd watched as more and more golf courses and gated communities encroached on farm and grazing land, and had begun to feel restless.

One day, while browsing through an industry journal, his gaze was drawn to an ad for a small-town veterinarian practice in the mountains near Reno, and for some reason the ad remained in his head for days afterwards. It had been on the July 4 weekend, just as the last of the fireworks were exploding in the star filled sky over the town square, when the notion had taken hold of him that he was going to answer that ad. Up until that instant Doc hadn't had a conscious thought about moving, but in that short moment, which took about the time an eye takes to blink, it was already decided. He'd had an epiphany, he supposed, and it felt too right to ignore.

Within the month, arrangements were made. He packed up, loaded his van with his chestnut mare, Lucky, and headed out. It was during that ride that the hole in his soul began to fill in, but he only realized that later. He remembered coming around a bend in the highway and being struck speechless by an impressive view of far-off mountain peaks and blue, blue sky, and zap! It was as though hot soup or warm milk began to invade his bloodstream, filling in all the blank spaces and the lonely pockets within him.

But there was more to the miracle.

Not five minutes later he'd come around another bend and happened upon...Cassie. When he gazed into her eyes that first time, it was right then that he experienced joy, more than that—elation—for the first time in his life.

Yet even with that great beginning, it had not been all wonder and contentment after that. No, there had been some adjusting to do. There'd been all that Cowboy Charlie stuff they'd had to get through. From the start of their relationship, Doc heard the tale about the magic glasses and the one wish and Cowboy Charlie's sudden appearance. And from what others said, there were some real similarities between him and this Charlie person, not just physical characteristics, but the fact that they had the same first name, as did their horses: Felicity—Charlie's horse—was Latin for Happy or Lucky—who was Doc's.

Cassie had been quick to point out the differences between Doc and the cowboy, too. Doc's eyes, while blue, had more of a greenish tinge to them, and a childhood accident had given him a slightly off-center bump on the bridge of his nose. Doc wore glasses to read and his hair was a bit darker.

He'd listened to her story, he knew that she believed with all her heart that somehow Charlie had been reincarnated or soul-traded or some such nonsense into Doc, but he wasn't buying it. He was a trained scientist, after all, and tended to give credence more to coincidence than magic. Even when he thought about the events that led him to Nevada, and the sudden shift in his insides not five minutes before meeting Cassie, even the astonishing sense of coming home he'd had when he'd looked into her eyes, well, sure it made him think. But that was all. He wasn't closed to possibilities, just doubtful. He could accept the word fate, if pushed. But magic? Not likely.

After a few weeks of wrangling, they'd agreed to disagree, because they agreed on so much else, the important stuff, like respect for each other and being a responsible member of society, and providing Trish with a sense of safety, the knowledge that she would always be loved. If Cowboy Charlie had existed—and Doc still got a twist of jealousy in his gut at the thought, although it lessened as time went on—well, the man was no longer around. Comparisons were an exercise in futility. Cassie was his now.

As she finished reading the selection from her first full length novel, *The Day Cowboy Charlie Became Real,* Cassie removed her reading glasses, the same hideous turquoise-and-rhinestone creations that had begun the whole thing. There was enthusiastic applause from those who had gathered to hear her, and she smiled her thanks. Doc watched as she signed books, something she seemed to still got a kick out of, even though, with two previous collections of children's stories released in the last year, she'd been doing it for a while now.

That warm soup feeling spread over him, taking him by surprise, as it always did. God, he loved her!

He remembered the night he'd said the words for the first time. Not just to her, but to anyone. It was about two months after they'd met. He'd been over for dinner, and Trish had gone off to watch her favorite TV show.

Since meeting, Cassie and Doc had been pretty inseparable, but on this night, he sat at the table sipping coffee. Instead of clearing it, as she usually did, she'd walked over to him and stood facing him. There'd been a look in her eyes as she'd swiped some hair off his brow and said he needed a haircut, a look that had made his heart turn over.

"What?" he said softly, but she didn't answer, so he pressed it. "Why are you looking at me that way?"

She shook her head, frowned. Then she'd smiled, and if it could be said that a smile was both gut-wrenchingly sad and filled with wonder at the same time, then that was Cassie's smile.

"I just realized," she said, then swallowed before she went on. "Charlie is well and truly gone now, and you're here instead."

He felt a lump in his own throat. "Do you miss him?"

She squatted and rested her hands on his knees. "No, not really," she said, gazing up at him through eyes that were suddenly bright with moisture. "It's kind of like I had a dream once, a wonderful dream, but that was all it was. A dream about a man who couldn't survive in this century. You're different. You're real. I mean, you didn't spring up out of nowhere, you had a life before you met me—"

"Half a life." He interrupted the flow of words, gazing down on her, cupping her cheeks in his hands.

"A life spent waiting for you." He swallowed the lump in his throat and managed to get the words out. "I love you, you know."

"Oh." Her eyes widened with surprise, then tears, one after the other, slid slowly down over her cheeks. "I'm so glad you do, because I love you, too. You, Doc, only you."

Reaching for her, Doc drew her up and onto his lap sideways, so that her legs dangled over his right thigh. He pulled her tight to him, and she buried her face in his neck. He felt the moisture of her tears against his skin and as he stroked her hair, he thought if time were to stop right then, it couldn't have picked a more perfect moment to do so.

"You're a miracle," he told her as she sniffled into his neck.

"No," she said, her chest heaving in quick, stuttering little movements against him, "we are."

As she signed her name on the flyleaf, Cassie felt a faint stirring in her belly. Covering her rounded stomach with her hand, she silently told her next child to wait to turn over, if possible, for a half hour or so. She patted him and he stilled. Good boy, she thought, do what you're told.

Although if he was anything like his father, she doubted he'd keep still or do as he was told. She had married a strong man with a mind of his own. They fought some and made up beautifully, and Cassie could honestly say she was as happy in her marriage to Dr. Charles McMasters as she'd ever dreamed it was possible to be. He was just enough like Cowboy Charlie to make her believe in magic, but his own man, too, so he could still surprise her. And did so, often.

It was good, she thought, inhaling the deep breath of a woman with blessings. Life was good. Life was better than good. It was lovely.

As she signed her name, she took a moment to chat with each person who had been kind enough to buy one of her books. At the end of the line was the tall, skinny, awkward-looking young woman who owned the bookstore. As she presented her own copy to be signed, she pointed to the reading glasses that lay on the table by Cassie's pens.

"Cool specs," the young woman said. "Where'd you get them?"

"That's kind of a long story, Gerri."

"Oh, okay." She made a face of self-reproach, as though kicking herself for speaking up.

"I'll tell it to you sometime, if you'd like."

When Gerri's face lit up with pleasure, the strangest urge came over Cassie, so she followed through on it. Smiling, she offered the glasses to her. "Here."

Her mouth dropped open with surprise. "For me?"

"Take them," Cassie told her, then turned her head to gaze at her husband. A look of such deep love passed between them that she thought the entire world could read it. "They're magic, you know," she said to the young woman, all the while keeping her eyes locked on Doc. "And I don't need magic anymore."

* * * * *

Silhouette Romance introduces tales of enchanted love and things beyond explanation in the new series

Soulmates

Couples destined for each other are brought together by the powerful magic of love....

A precious gift brings
A HUSBAND IN HER EYES
by Karen Rose Smith (on sale March 2002)

Dreams come true in
CASSIE'S COWBOY
by Diane Pershing (on sale April 2002)

A legacy of love arrives
BECAUSE OF THE RING
by Stella Bagwell (on sale May 2002)

Available at your favorite retail outlet.

Silhouette®
Where love comes alive™

Visit Silhouette at www.eHarlequin.com
SRSOUL

Silhouette presents an exciting new continuity series:

CROWN AND GLORY

When a royal family rolls out the red carpet for love, power and deception, will their lives change forever?

The saga begins in April 2002 with:
The Princess Is Pregnant!
by Laurie Paige (SE #1459)

**May: THE PRINCESS AND THE DUKE by Allison Leigh
(SE #1465)**

**June: ROYAL PROTOCOL by Christine Flynn
(SE #1471)**

Be sure to catch all nine Crown and Glory stories: the first three appear in Silhouette Special Edition, the next three continue in Silhouette Romance and the saga concludes with three books in Silhouette Desire.

And be sure not to miss more royal stories, from Silhouette Intimate Moments'

Romancing the Crown,
running January through December.

Silhouette
Where love comes alive™

Available at your favorite retail outlet.

Visit Silhouette at www.eHarlequin.com

SSECAG

April 2002 brings four dark and captivating paranormal romances in which the promise of passion, mystery and suspense await…

Experience the dark side of love with

Silhouette DREAMSCAPES

WATCHING FOR WILLA
by *USA Today* bestselling author Helen R. Myers

DARK MOON
by Lindsay Longford

THIS TIME FOREVER
by Meg Chittenden

WAITING FOR THE WOLF MOON
by Evelyn Vaughn

Coming to a store near you in April 2002.

Silhouette
Where love comes alive™

Visit Silhouette at www.eHarlequin.com

RCDREAM6

If you enjoyed what you just read,
then we've got an offer you can't resist!

Take 2 bestselling love stories FREE!

Plus get a FREE surprise gift!

Clip this page and mail it to Silhouette Reader Service™

IN U.S.A.	IN CANADA
3010 Walden Ave.	P.O. Box 609
P.O. Box 1867	Fort Erie, Ontario
Buffalo, N.Y. 14240-1867	L2A 5X3

YES! Please send me 2 free Silhouette Romance® novels and my free surprise gift. After receiving them, if I don't wish to receive anymore, I can return the shipping statement marked cancel. If I don't cancel, I will receive 6 brand-new novels every month, before they're available in stores! In the U.S.A., bill me at the bargain price of $3.15 plus 25¢ shipping and handling per book and applicable sales tax, if any*. In Canada, bill me at the bargain price of $3.50 plus 25¢ shipping and handling per book and applicable taxes**. That's the complete price and a savings of at least 10% off the cover prices—what a great deal! I understand that accepting the 2 free books and gift places me under no obligation ever to buy any books. I can always return a shipment and cancel at any time. Even if I never buy another book from Silhouette, the 2 free books and gift are mine to keep forever.

215 SEN DFNQ
315 SEN DFNR

Name	(PLEASE PRINT)	
Address	Apt.#	
City	State/Prov.	Zip/Postal Code

* Terms and prices subject to change without notice. Sales tax applicable in N.Y.
** Canadian residents will be charged applicable provincial taxes and GST.
All orders subject to approval. Offer limited to one per household and not valid to current Silhouette Romance® subscribers.
® are registered trademarks of Harlequin Enterprises Limited.

SROM01 ©1998 Harlequin Enterprises Limited

King Philippe has died, leaving no male heirs to ascend the throne. Until his mother announces that a son *may* exist, embarking everyone on a desperate search for... the missing heir.

Their quest begins March 2002 and continues through June 2002.

On sale March 2002, the emotional
OF ROYAL BLOOD
by Carolyn Zane (SR #1576)

On sale April 2002, the intense
IN PURSUIT OF A PRINCESS
by Donna Clayton (SR #1582)

On sale May 2002, the heartwarming
A PRINCESS IN WAITING
by Carol Grace (SR #1588)

On sale June 2002, the exhilarating
A PRINCE AT LAST!
by Cathie Linz (SR #1594)

Available at your favorite retail outlet.

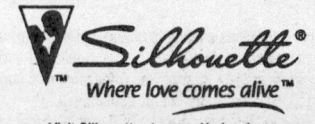

Silhouette®
Where love comes alive™

Visit Silhouette at www.eHarlequin.com
SRRW4

eHARLEQUIN.com

| community | membership |
| buy books | authors | online reads | magazine | learn to write |

buy books
♥ We have your favorite books from Harlequin, Silhouette, MIRA and Steeple Hill, plus bestselling authors in Other Romances. Discover savings, find new releases and fall in love with past classics all over again!

online reads
♥ Read daily and weekly chapters from Internet-exclusive serials, and decide what should happen next in great interactive stories!

magazine
♥ Learn how to spice up your love life, play fun games and quizzes, read about celebrities, travel, beauty and so much more.

authors
♥ Select from over 300 author profiles and read interviews with your favorite bestselling authors!

community
♥ Share your passion for love, life and romance novels in our online message boards!

learn to write
♥ All the tips and tools you need to craft the perfect novel, including our special romance novel critique service.

membership
♥ FREE! Be the first to hear about all your favorite themes, authors and series and be part of exciting contests, exclusive promotions, special deals and online events.

Silhouette®

Where love comes alive™—online...

Visit us at
www.eHarlequin.com

SINT7CH

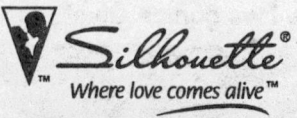